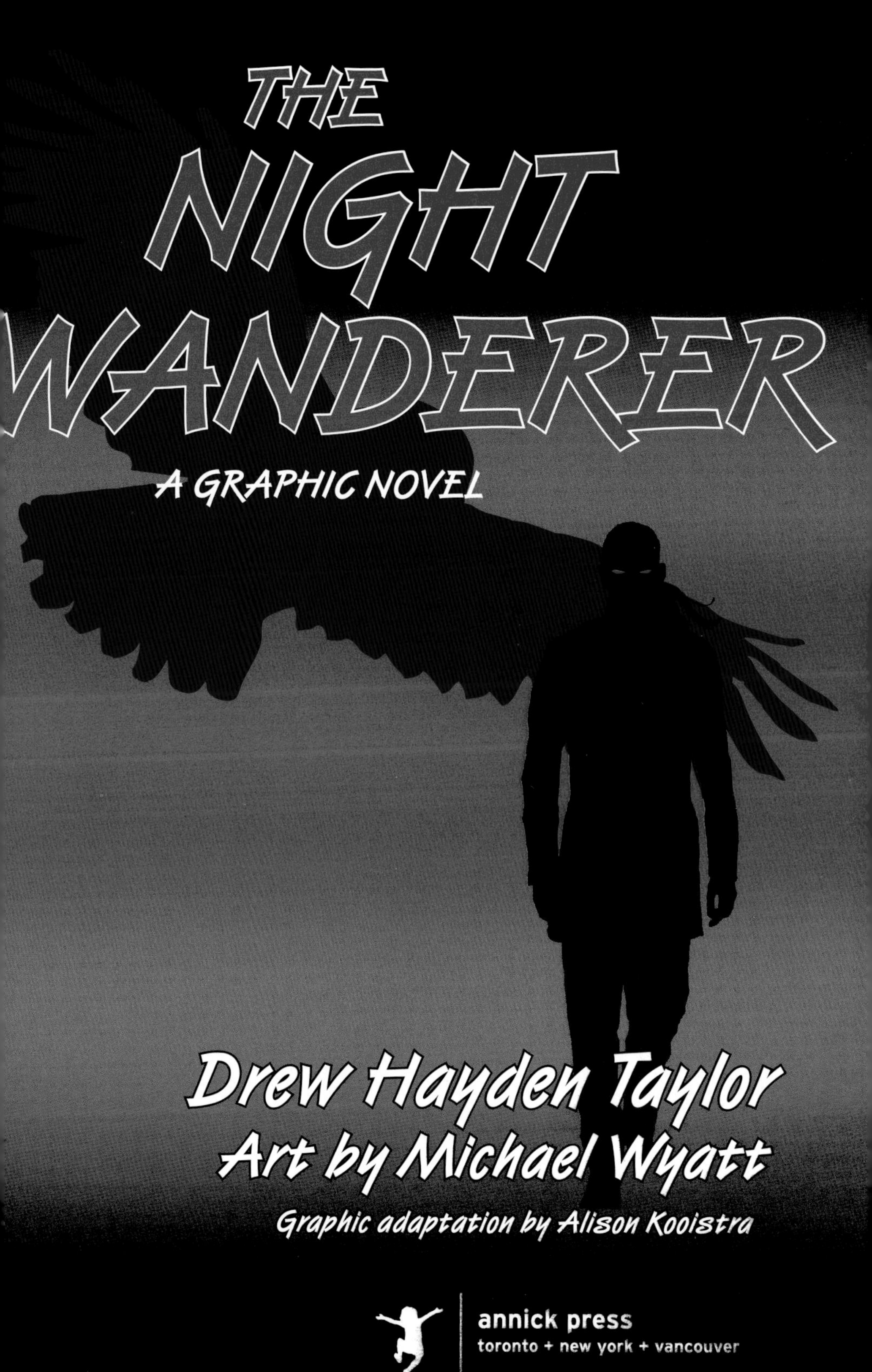

THE NIGHT WANDERER

A GRAPHIC NOVEL

Drew Hayden Taylor

Art by Michael Wyatt

Graphic adaptation by Alison Kooistra

annick press

toronto + new york + vancouver

Graphic novel adaptation by Alison Kooistra
Based on the novel *The Night Wanderer: A Native Gothic Novel*, © 2007 Drew Hayden Taylor
Cover art by Michael Wyatt
Cover design by Sheryl Shapiro
Proofread by Tanya Trafford

Annick Press Ltd.

We acknowledge the support of the Canada Council for the Arts, the Ontario Arts Council, and the Government of Canada through the Canada Book Fund (CBF) for our publishing activities.

ONTARIO ARTS COUNCIL
CONSEIL DES ARTS DE L'ONTARIO
50 YEARS OF ONTARIO GOVERNMENT SUPPORT OF THE ARTS
50 ANS DE SOUTIEN DU GOUVERNEMENT DE L'ONTARIO AUX ARTS

Cataloging in Publication
Taylor, Drew Hayden, 1962-
    The night wanderer : a graphic novel / by Drew Hayden Taylor; art by Michael Wyatt ; graphic adaptation by Alison Kooistra.

Adaptation of the novel: The night wanderer.
Issued also in electronic formats.
ISBN 978-1-55451-573-8 (bound).—ISBN 978-1-55451-572-1 (pbk.)

    1. Graphic novels. I. Wyatt, Mike, 1966- II. Kooistra, Alison, 1979- III. Taylor, Drew Hayden, 1962- . Night wanderer. IV. Title.

PN6733.T39N54 2013   j741.5'971   C2013-901752-6

Printed and bound in China.
Published in the U.S.A. by Annick Press (U.S.) Ltd.

Distributed in Canada by
Firefly Books Ltd.
50 Staples Avenue, Unit 1
Richmond Hill, ON
L4B 0A7

Distributed in the U.S.A. by
Firefly Books (U.S.) Inc.
P.O. Box 1338
Ellicott Station
Buffalo, NY 14205

Visit us at: **www.annickpress.com**
Visit Drew Hayden Taylor at: **www.drewhaydentaylor.com**
Visit Michael Wyatt at: **mgwyatt.blogspot.ca**

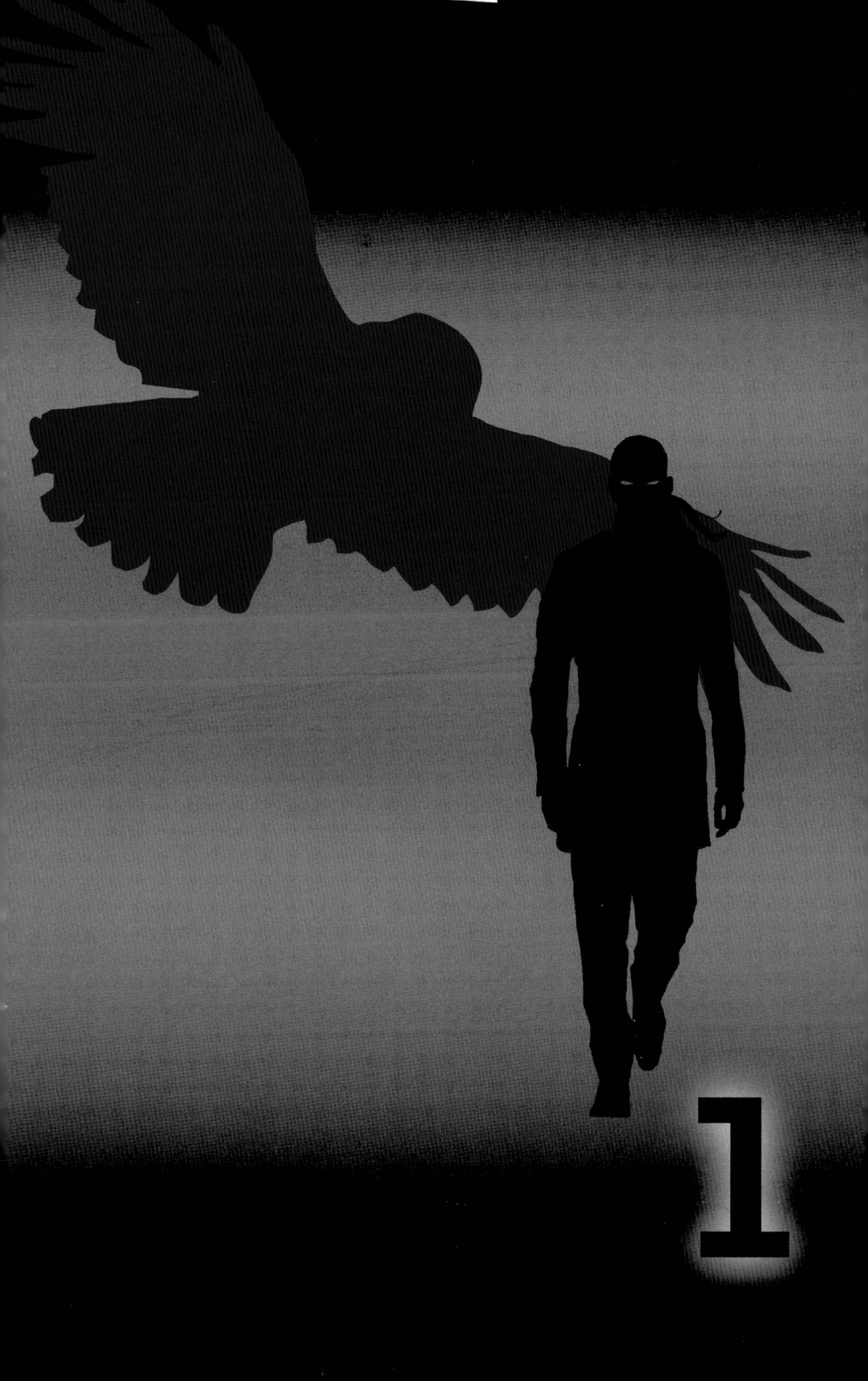
1

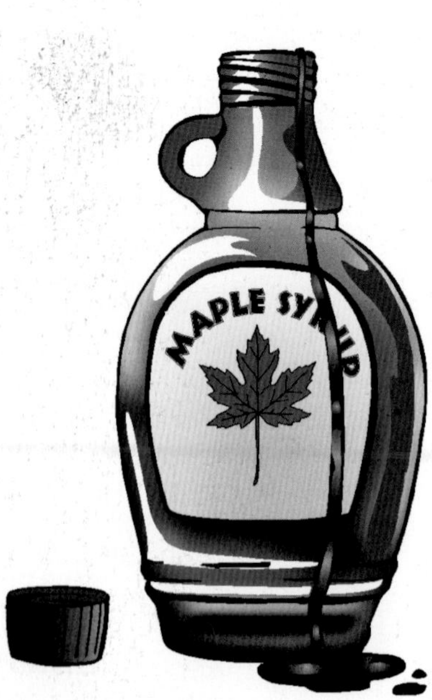
MAPLE SY

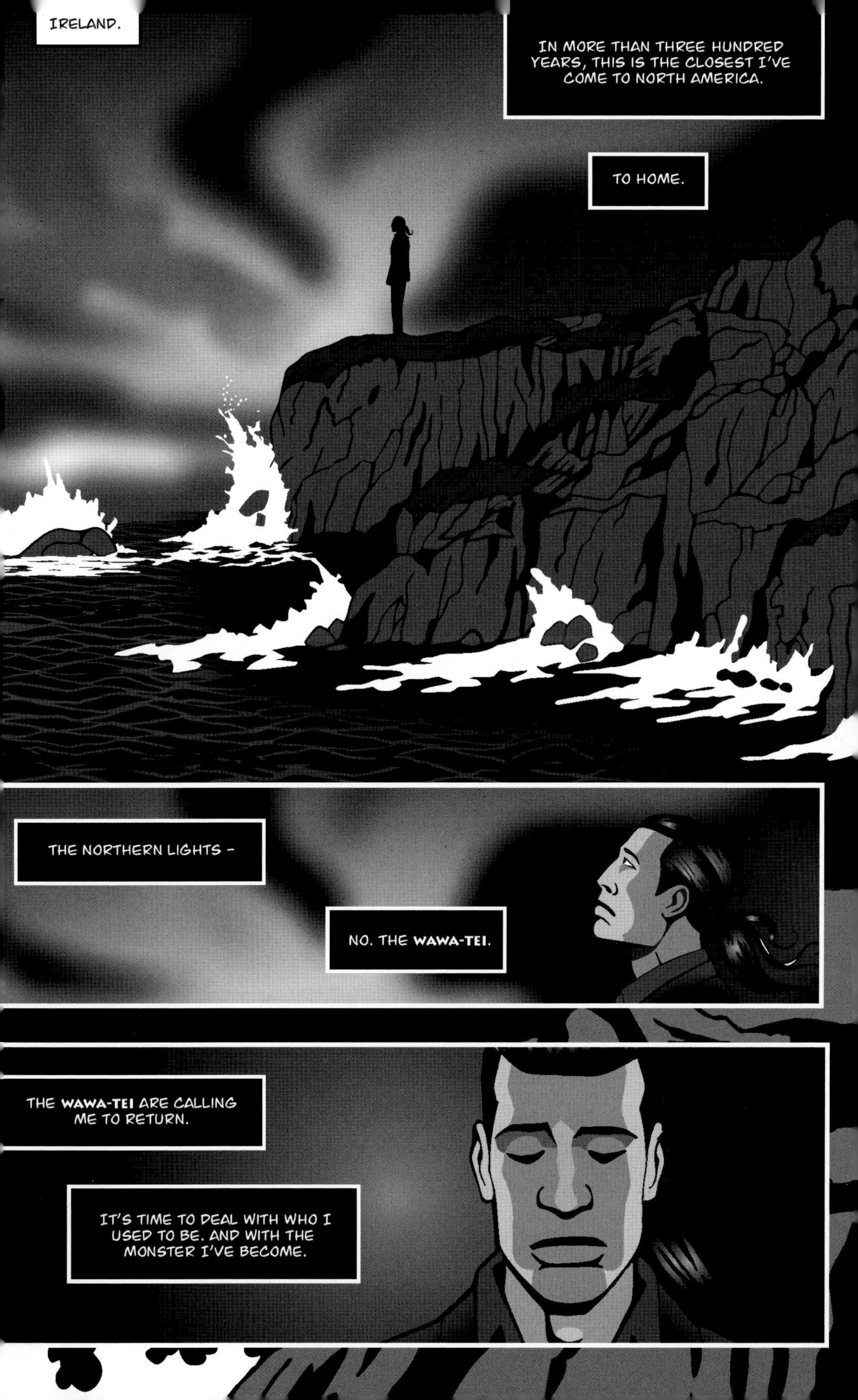
IRELAND.
IN MORE THAN THREE HUNDRED YEARS, THIS IS THE CLOSEST I'VE COME TO NORTH AMERICA.
TO HOME.
THE NORTHERN LIGHTS –
NO. THE **WAWA-TEI**.
THE **WAWA-TEI** ARE CALLING ME TO RETURN.
IT'S TIME TO DEAL WITH WHO I USED TO BE. AND WITH THE MONSTER I'VE BECOME.

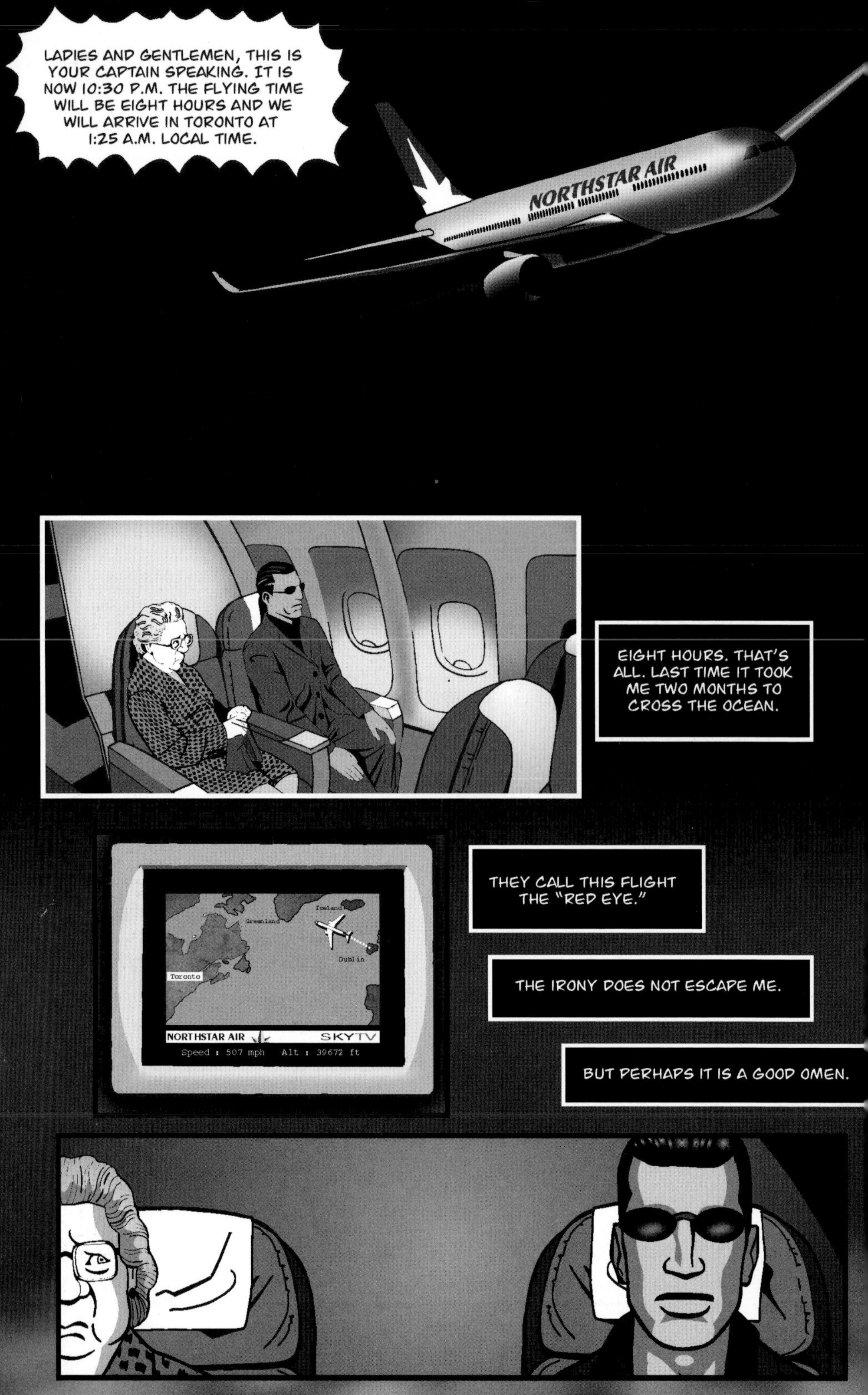
LADIES AND GENTLEMEN, THIS IS YOUR CAPTAIN SPEAKING. IT IS NOW 10:30 P.M. THE FLYING TIME WILL BE EIGHT HOURS AND WE WILL ARRIVE IN TORONTO AT 1:25 A.M. LOCAL TIME.
NORTHSTAR AIR
EIGHT HOURS. THAT'S ALL. LAST TIME IT TOOK ME TWO MONTHS TO CROSS THE OCEAN.
Iceland
Greenland
Dublin
Toronto
NORTHSTAR AIR
SKYTV
Speed : 507 mph Alt : 39672 ft
THEY CALL THIS FLIGHT THE "RED EYE."
THE IRONY DOES NOT ESCAPE ME.
BUT PERHAPS IT IS A GOOD OMEN.

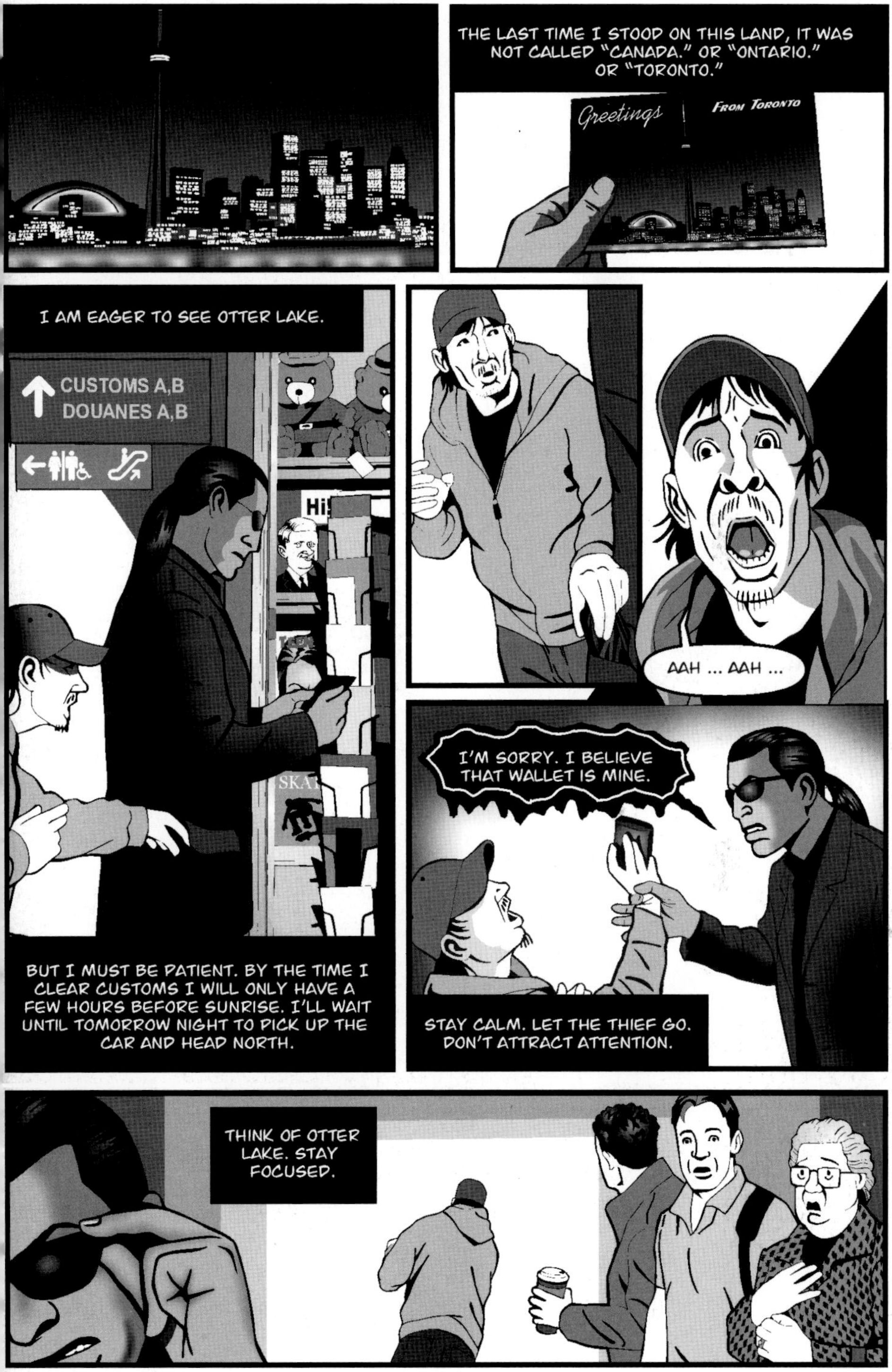
THE LAST TIME I STOOD ON THIS LAND, IT WAS NOT CALLED "CANADA." OR "ONTARIO." OR "TORONTO."
Greetings
FROM TORONTO
I AM EAGER TO SEE OTTER LAKE.
CUSTOMS A,B
DOUANES A,B
AAH ... AAH ...
I'M SORRY. I BELIEVE THAT WALLET IS MINE.
BUT I MUST BE PATIENT. BY THE TIME I CLEAR CUSTOMS I WILL ONLY HAVE A FEW HOURS BEFORE SUNRISE. I'LL WAIT UNTIL TOMORROW NIGHT TO PICK UP THE CAR AND HEAD NORTH.
STAY CALM. LET THE THIEF GO. DON'T ATTRACT ATTENTION.
THINK OF OTTER LAKE. STAY FOCUSED.

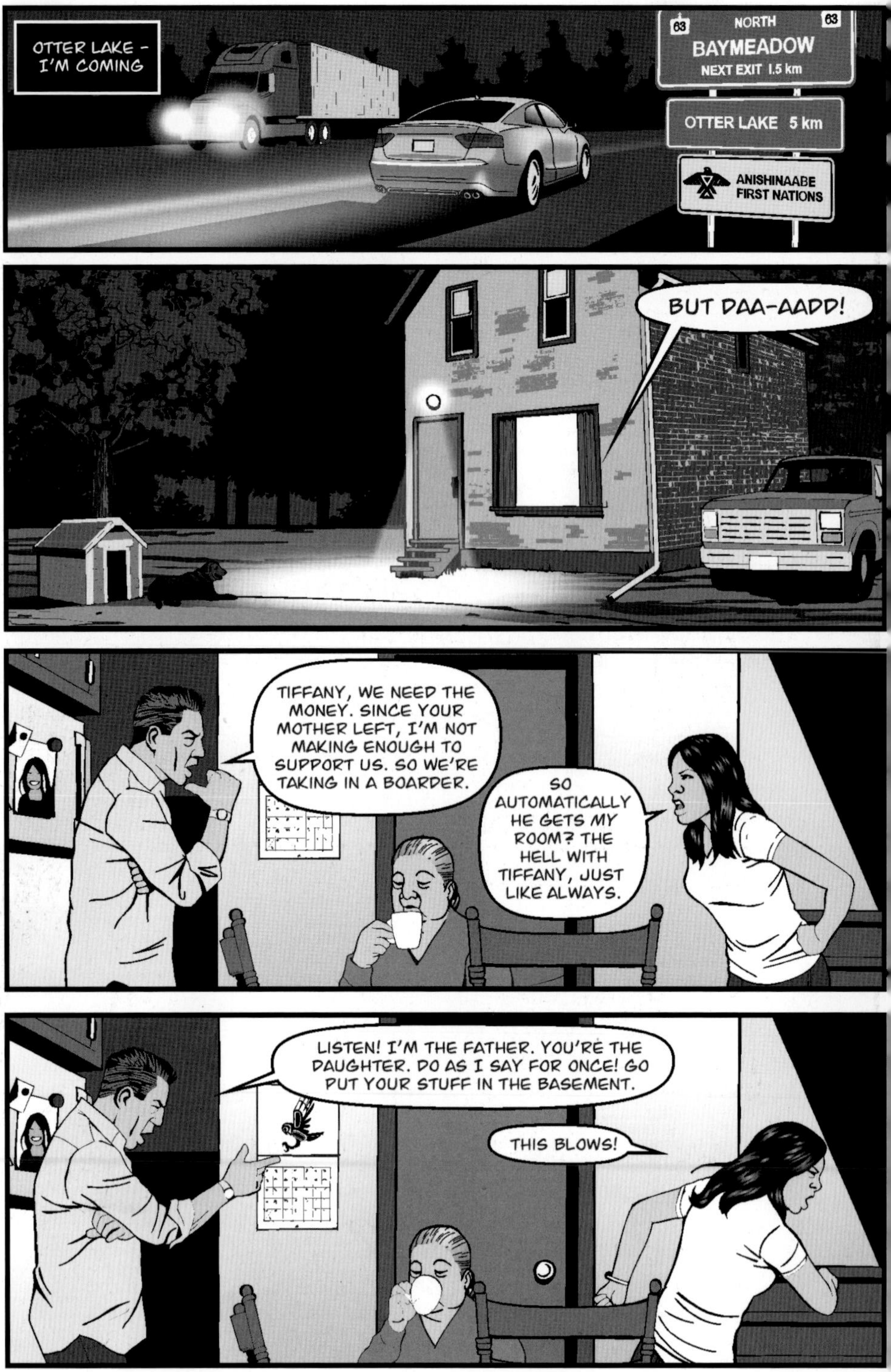
OTTER LAKE - I'M COMING
63 NORTH 63
BAYMEADOW
NEXT EXIT 1.5 km
OTTER LAKE 5 km
ANISHINAABE FIRST NATIONS
BUT DAA-AADD!
TIFFANY, WE NEED THE MONEY. SINCE YOUR MOTHER LEFT, I'M NOT MAKING ENOUGH TO SUPPORT US. SO WE'RE TAKING IN A BOARDER.
SO AUTOMATICALLY HE GETS MY ROOM? THE HELL WITH TIFFANY, JUST LIKE ALWAYS.
LISTEN! I'M THE FATHER. YOU'RE THE DAUGHTER. DO AS I SAY FOR ONCE! GO PUT YOUR STUFF IN THE BASEMENT.
THIS BLOWS!

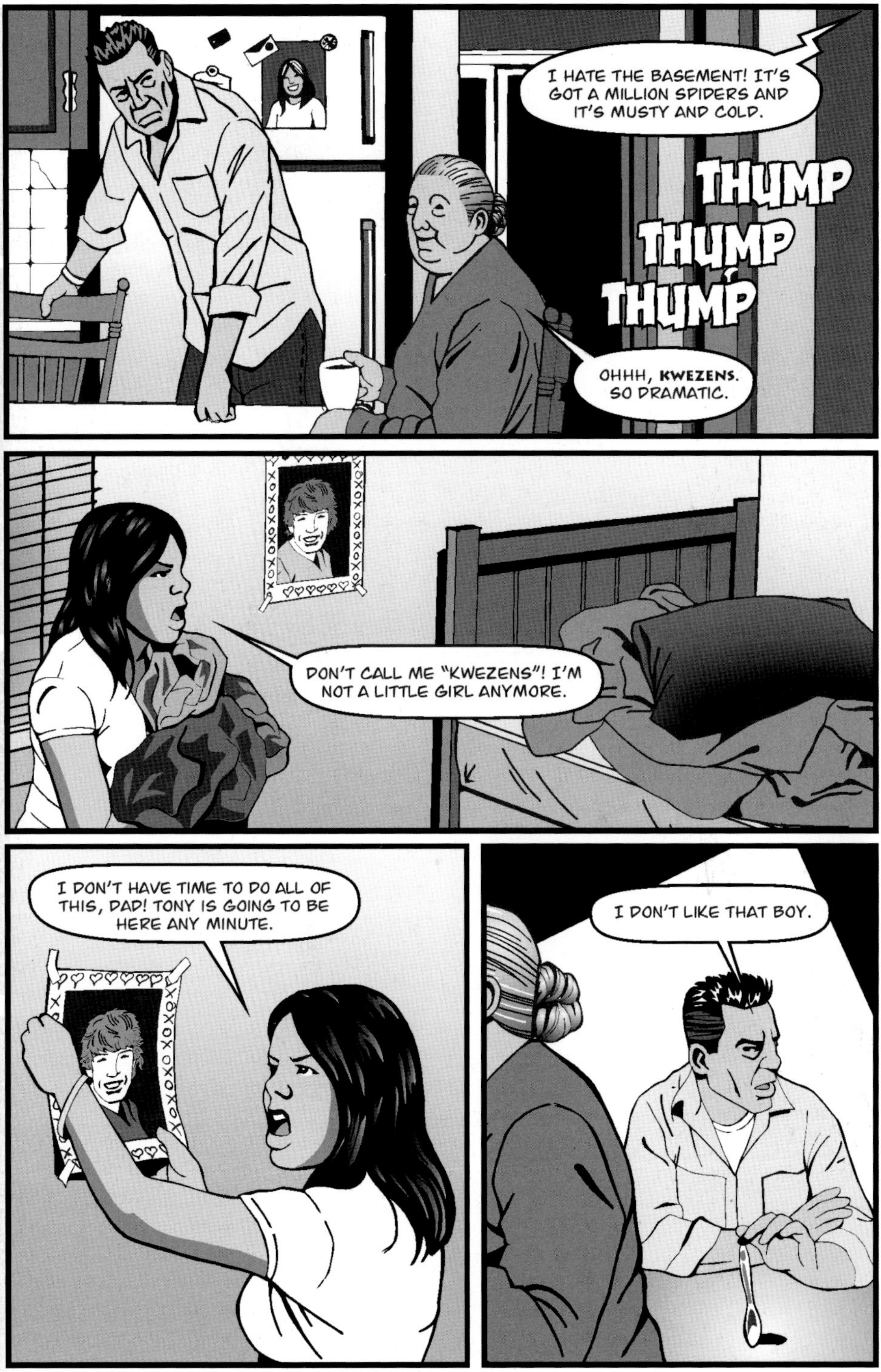
I HATE THE BASEMENT! IT'S GOT A MILLION SPIDERS AND IT'S MUSTY AND COLD.
THUMP THUMP THUMP
OHHH, **KWEZENS.** SO DRAMATIC.
DON'T CALL ME "KWEZENS"! I'M NOT A LITTLE GIRL ANYMORE.
I DON'T HAVE TIME TO DO ALL OF THIS, DAD! TONY IS GOING TO BE HERE ANY MINUTE.
I DON'T LIKE THAT BOY.

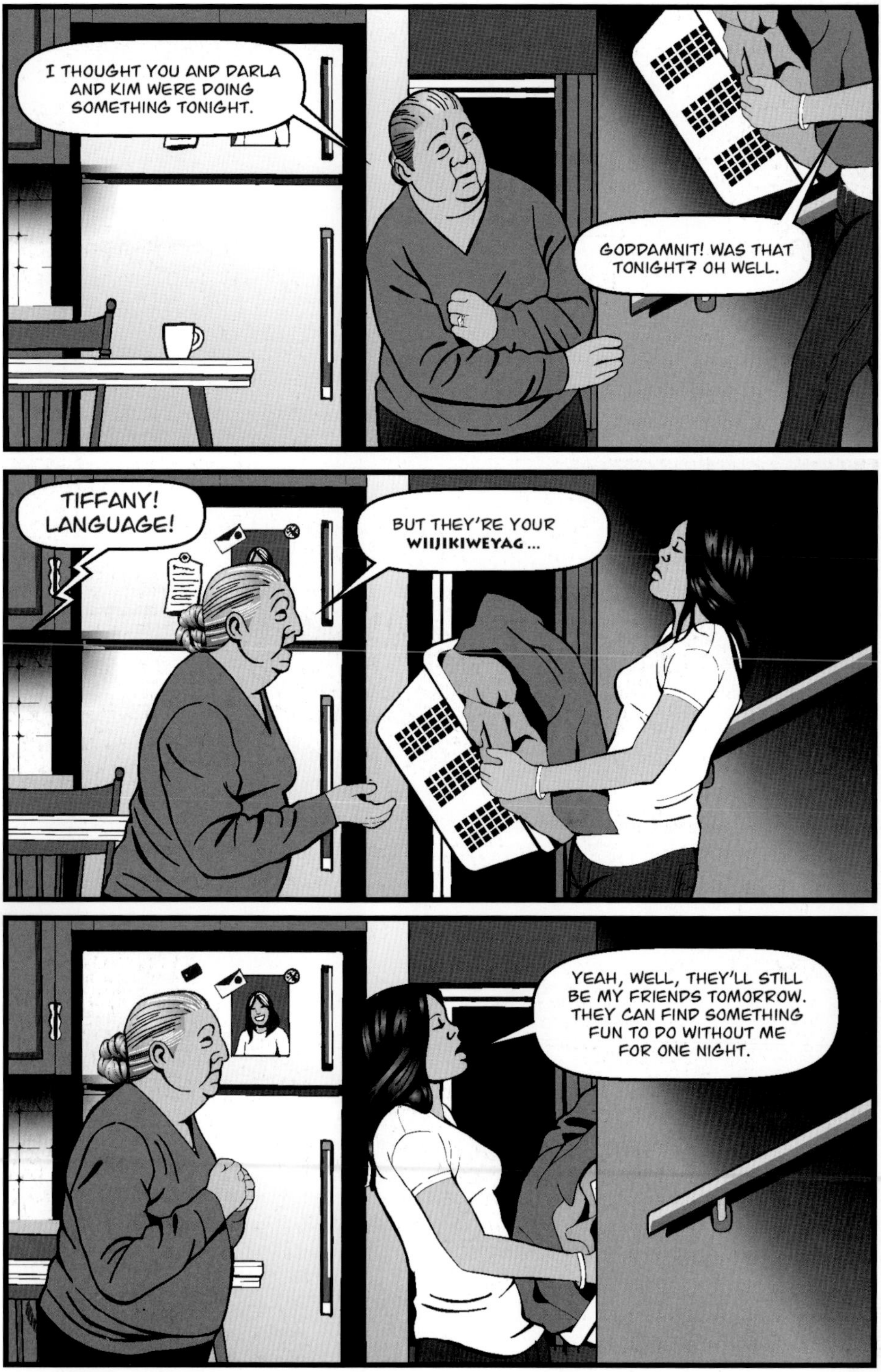

I THOUGHT YOU AND DARLA AND KIM WERE DOING SOMETHING TONIGHT.
GODDAMNIT! WAS THAT TONIGHT? OH WELL.
TIFFANY! LANGUAGE!
BUT THEY'RE YOUR WIIJIKIWEYAG ...
YEAH, WELL, THEY'LL STILL BE MY FRIENDS TOMORROW. THEY CAN FIND SOMETHING FUN TO DO WITHOUT ME FOR ONE NIGHT.

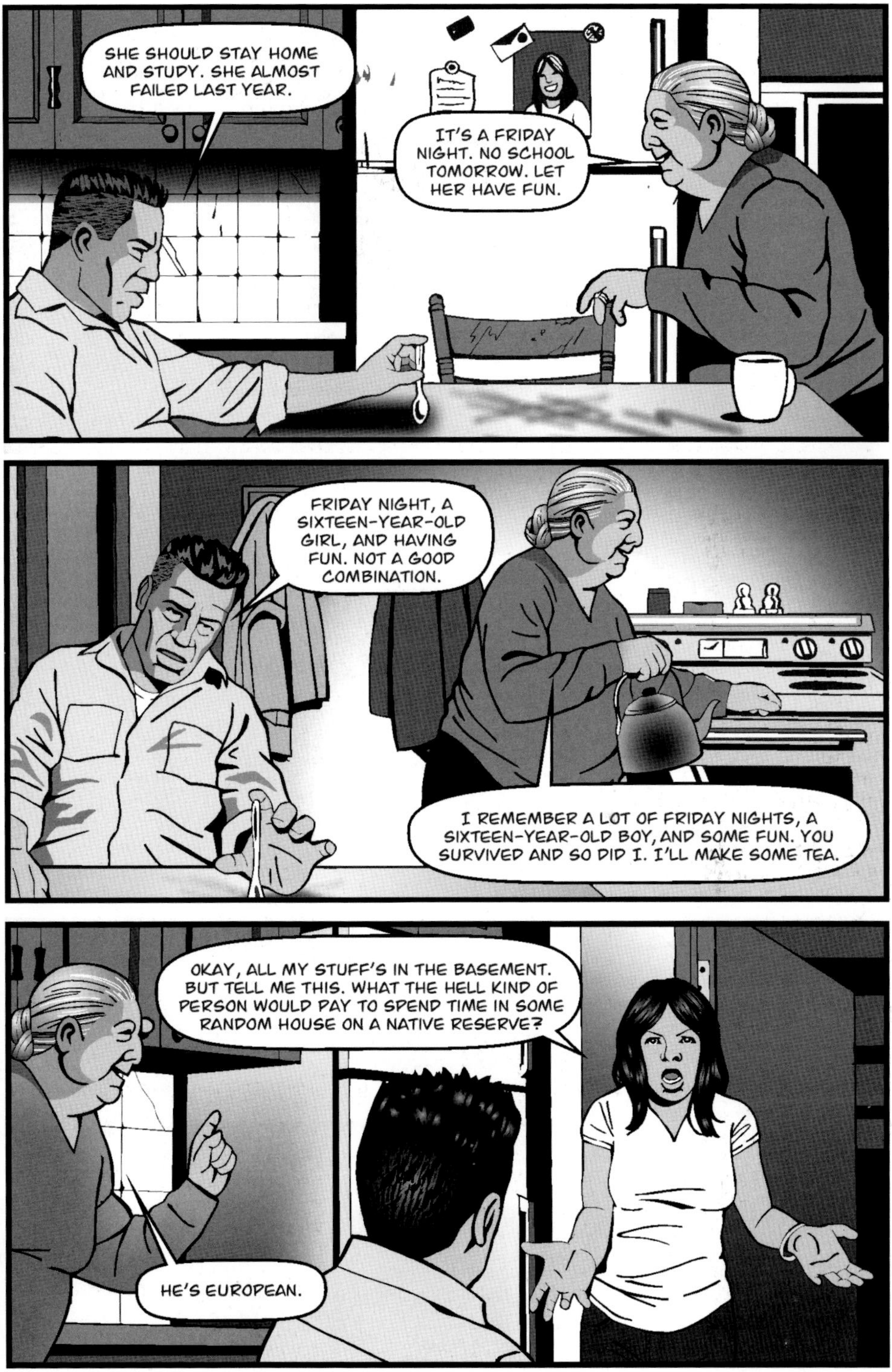
SHE SHOULD STAY HOME AND STUDY. SHE ALMOST FAILED LAST YEAR.
IT'S A FRIDAY NIGHT. NO SCHOOL TOMORROW. LET HER HAVE FUN.
FRIDAY NIGHT, A SIXTEEN-YEAR-OLD GIRL, AND HAVING FUN. NOT A GOOD COMBINATION.
I REMEMBER A LOT OF FRIDAY NIGHTS, A SIXTEEN-YEAR-OLD BOY, AND SOME FUN. YOU SURVIVED AND SO DID I. I'LL MAKE SOME TEA.
OKAY, ALL MY STUFF'S IN THE BASEMENT. BUT TELL ME THIS. WHAT THE HELL KIND OF PERSON WOULD PAY TO SPEND TIME IN SOME RANDOM HOUSE ON A NATIVE RESERVE?
HE'S EUROPEAN.

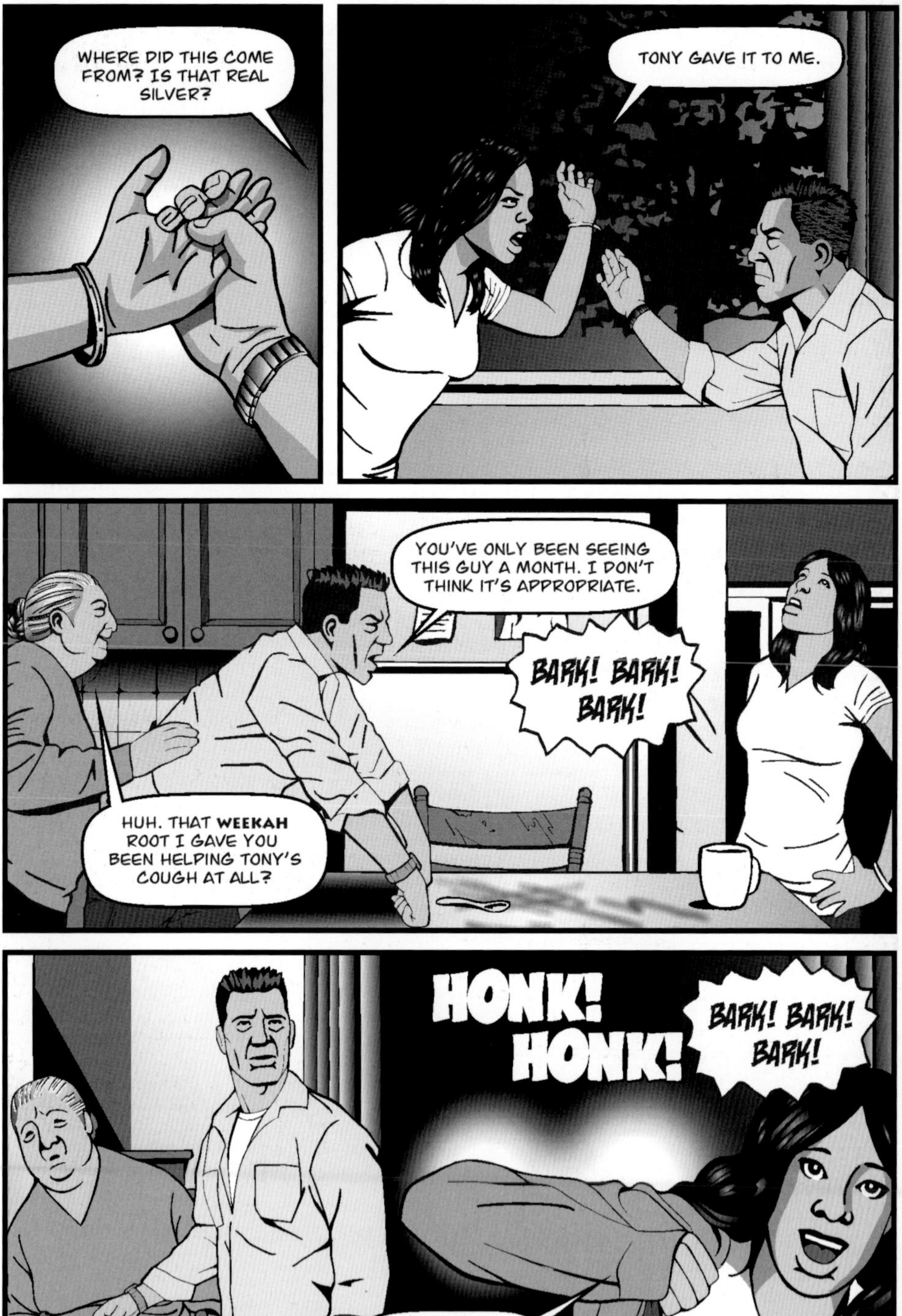
WHERE DID THIS COME FROM? IS THAT REAL SILVER?
TONY GAVE IT TO ME.
YOU'VE ONLY BEEN SEEING THIS GUY A MONTH. I DON'T THINK IT'S APPROPRIATE.
BARK! BARK! BARK!
HUH. THAT WEEKAH ROOT I GAVE YOU BEEN HELPING TONY'S COUGH AT ALL?
HONK! HONK!
BARK! BARK! BARK!
GOTTA GO!

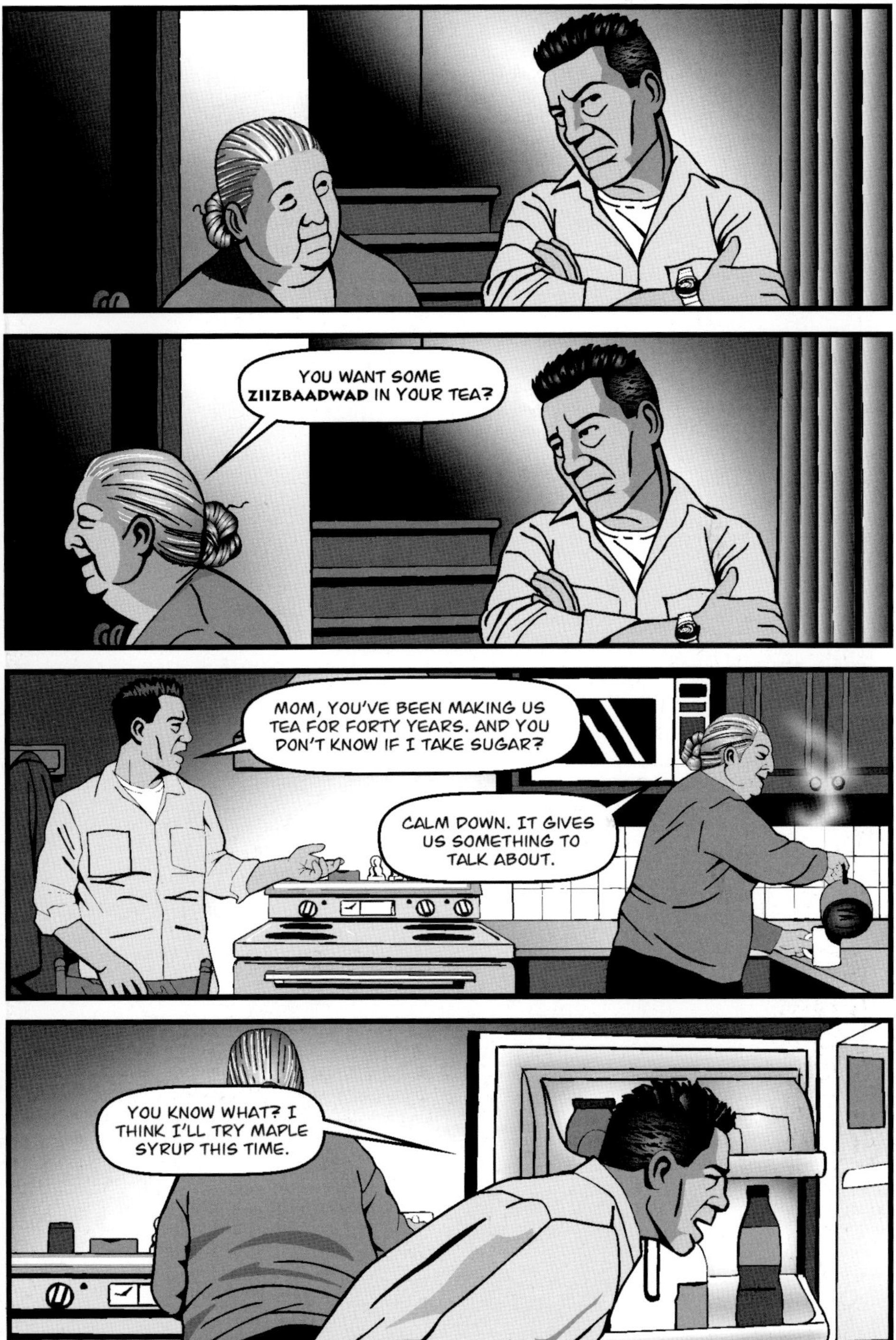
YOU WANT SOME ZIIZBAADWAD IN YOUR TEA?
MOM, YOU'VE BEEN MAKING US TEA FOR FORTY YEARS. AND YOU DON'T KNOW IF I TAKE SUGAR?
CALM DOWN. IT GIVES US SOMETHING TO TALK ABOUT.
YOU KNOW WHAT? I THINK I'LL TRY MAPLE SYRUP THIS TIME.

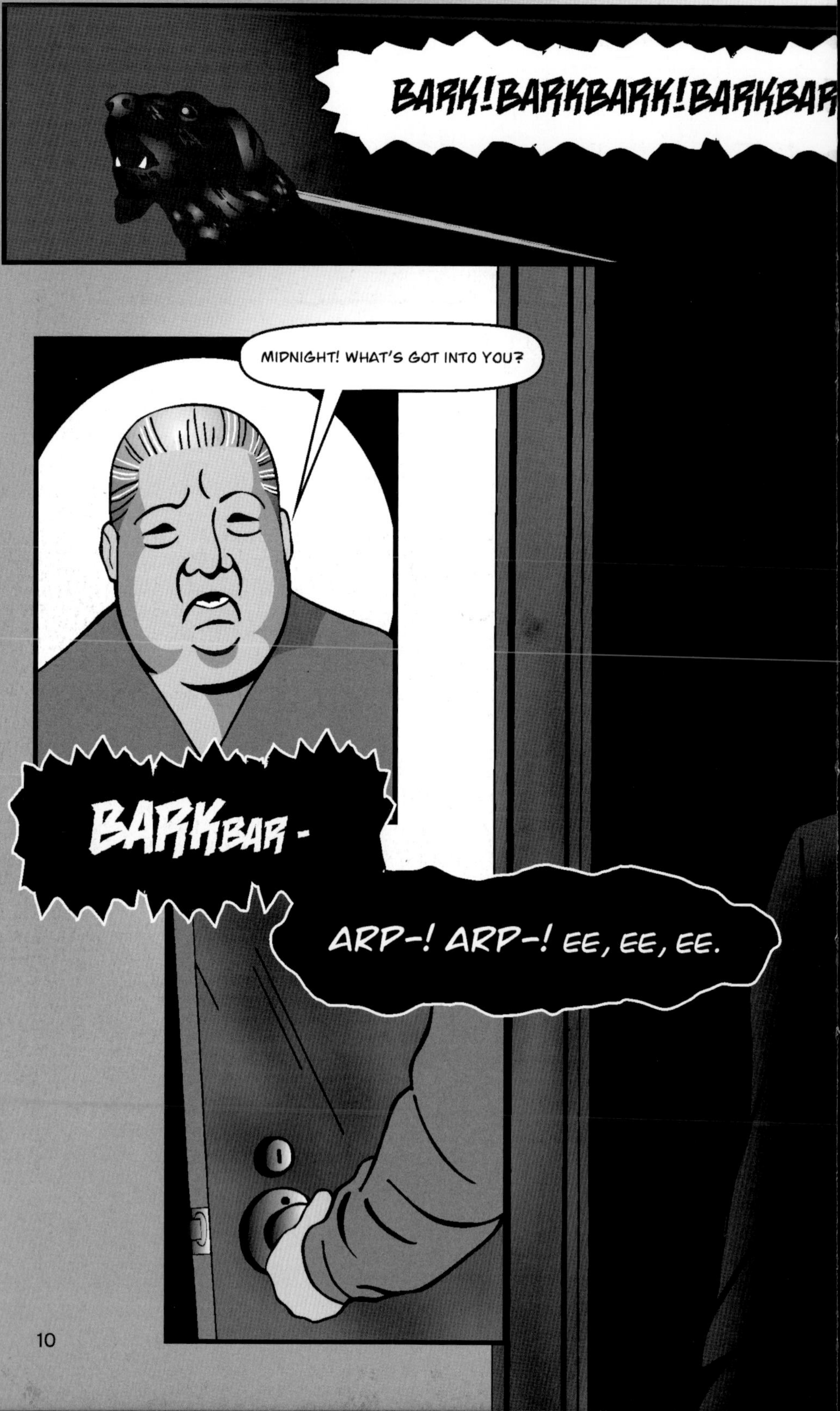
BARK!BARKBARK!BARKBAR
MIDNIGHT! WHAT'S GOT INTO YOU?
BARKBAR-
ARP-! ARP-! EE, EE, EE.

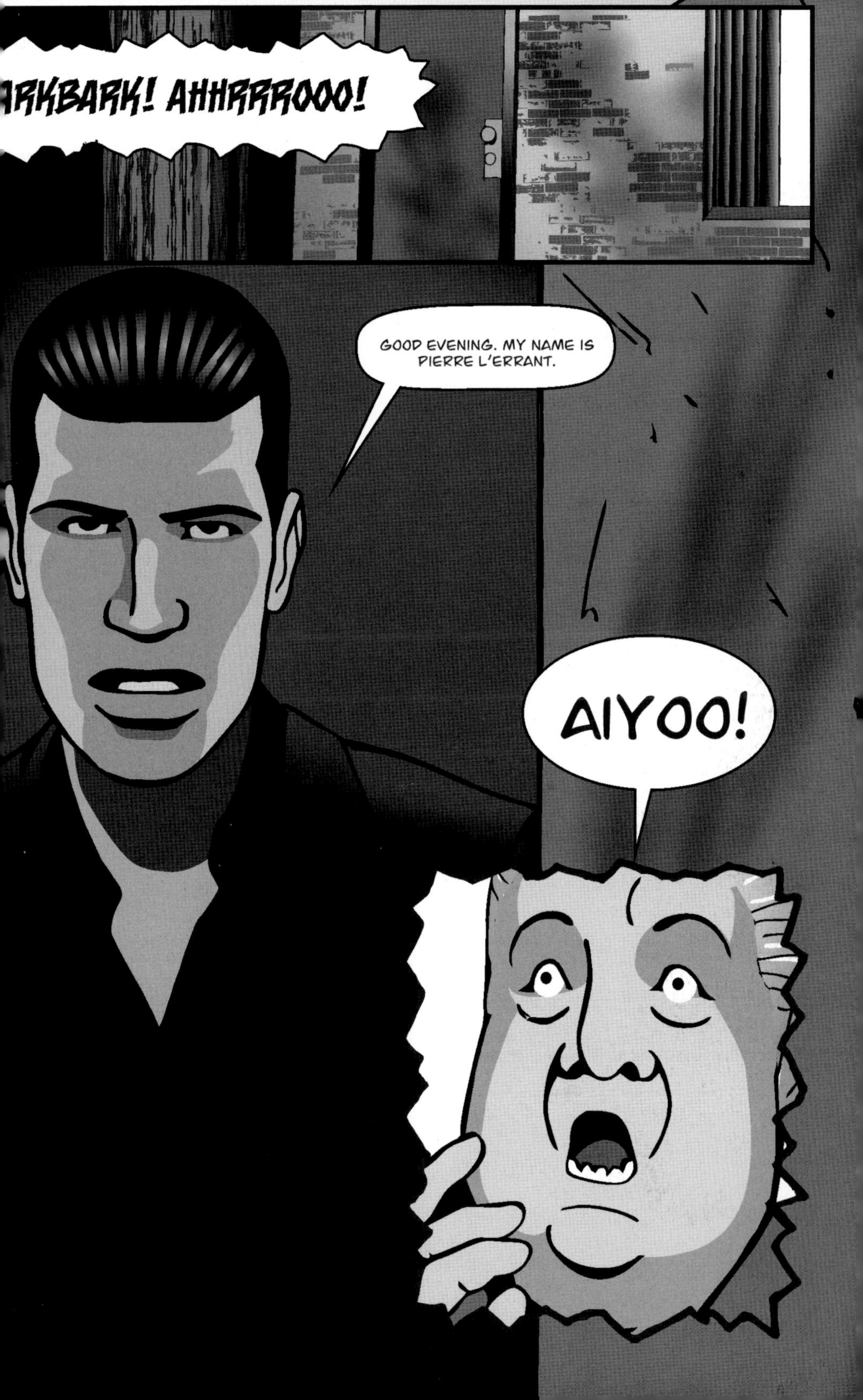
RKBARK! AHHRRROOO!
GOOD EVENING. MY NAME IS PIERRE L'ERRANT.
AIYOO!

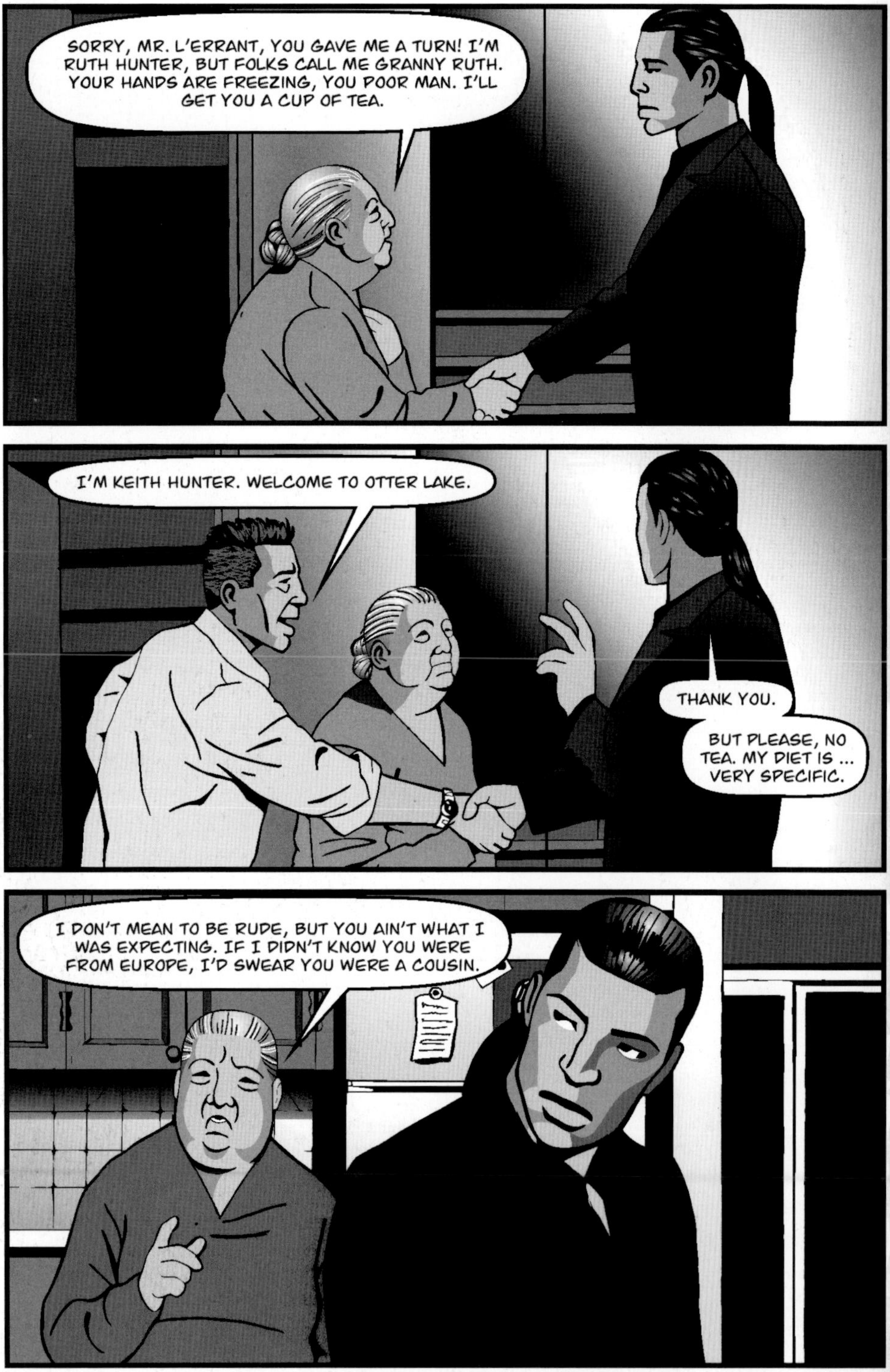
SORRY, MR. L'ERRANT, YOU GAVE ME A TURN! I'M RUTH HUNTER, BUT FOLKS CALL ME GRANNY RUTH. YOUR HANDS ARE FREEZING, YOU POOR MAN. I'LL GET YOU A CUP OF TEA.
I'M KEITH HUNTER. WELCOME TO OTTER LAKE.
THANK YOU.
BUT PLEASE, NO TEA. MY DIET IS ... VERY SPECIFIC.
I DON'T MEAN TO BE RUDE, BUT YOU AIN'T WHAT I WAS EXPECTING. IF I DIDN'T KNOW YOU WERE FROM EUROPE, I'D SWEAR YOU WERE A COUSIN.

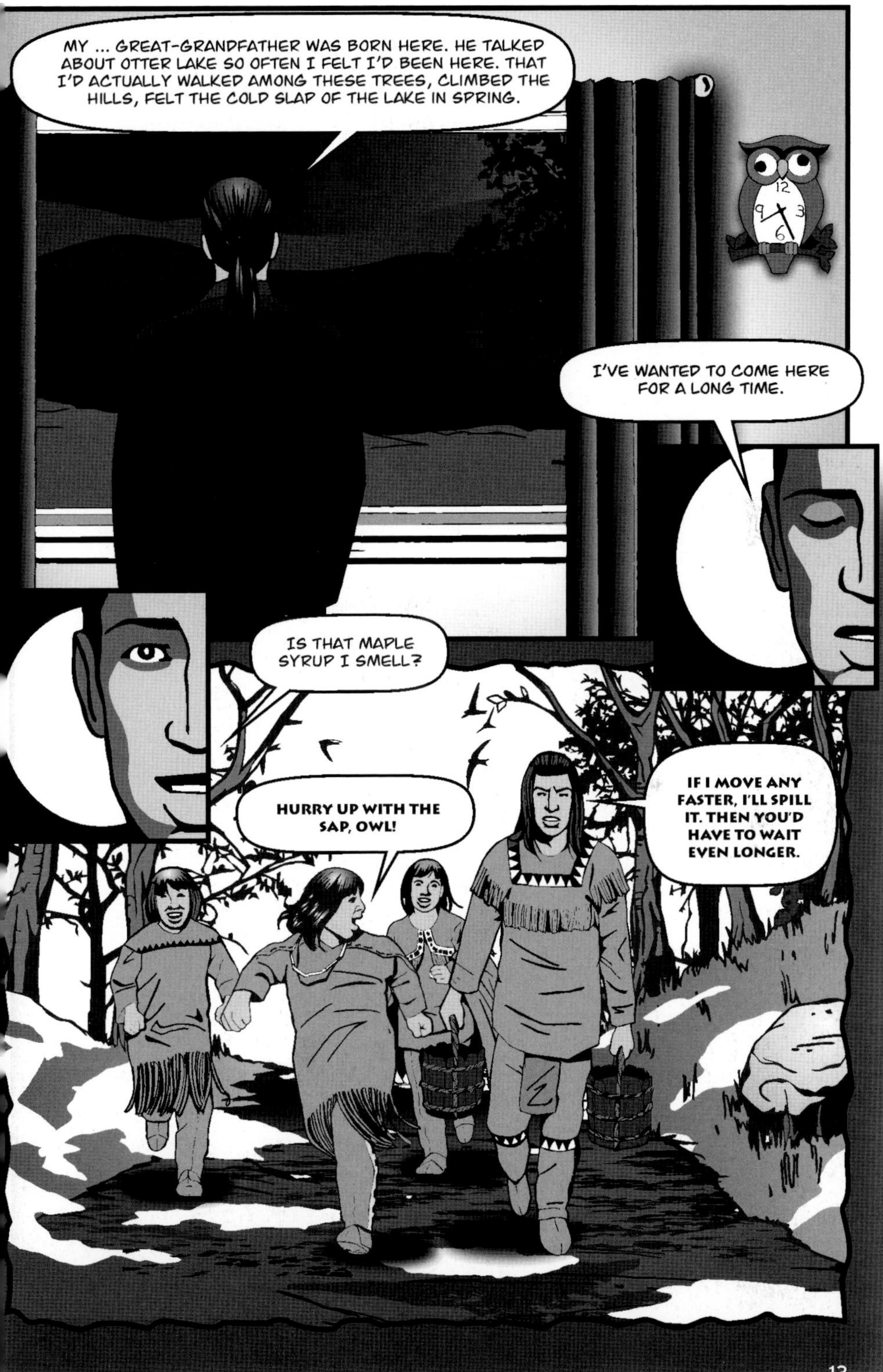
MY ... GREAT-GRANDFATHER WAS BORN HERE. HE TALKED ABOUT OTTER LAKE SO OFTEN I FELT I'D BEEN HERE. THAT I'D ACTUALLY WALKED AMONG THESE TREES, CLIMBED THE HILLS, FELT THE COLD SLAP OF THE LAKE IN SPRING.
I'VE WANTED TO COME HERE FOR A LONG TIME.
IS THAT MAPLE SYRUP I SMELL?
HURRY UP WITH THE SAP, OWL!
IF I MOVE ANY FASTER, I'LL SPILL IT. THEN YOU'D HAVE TO WAIT EVEN LONGER.

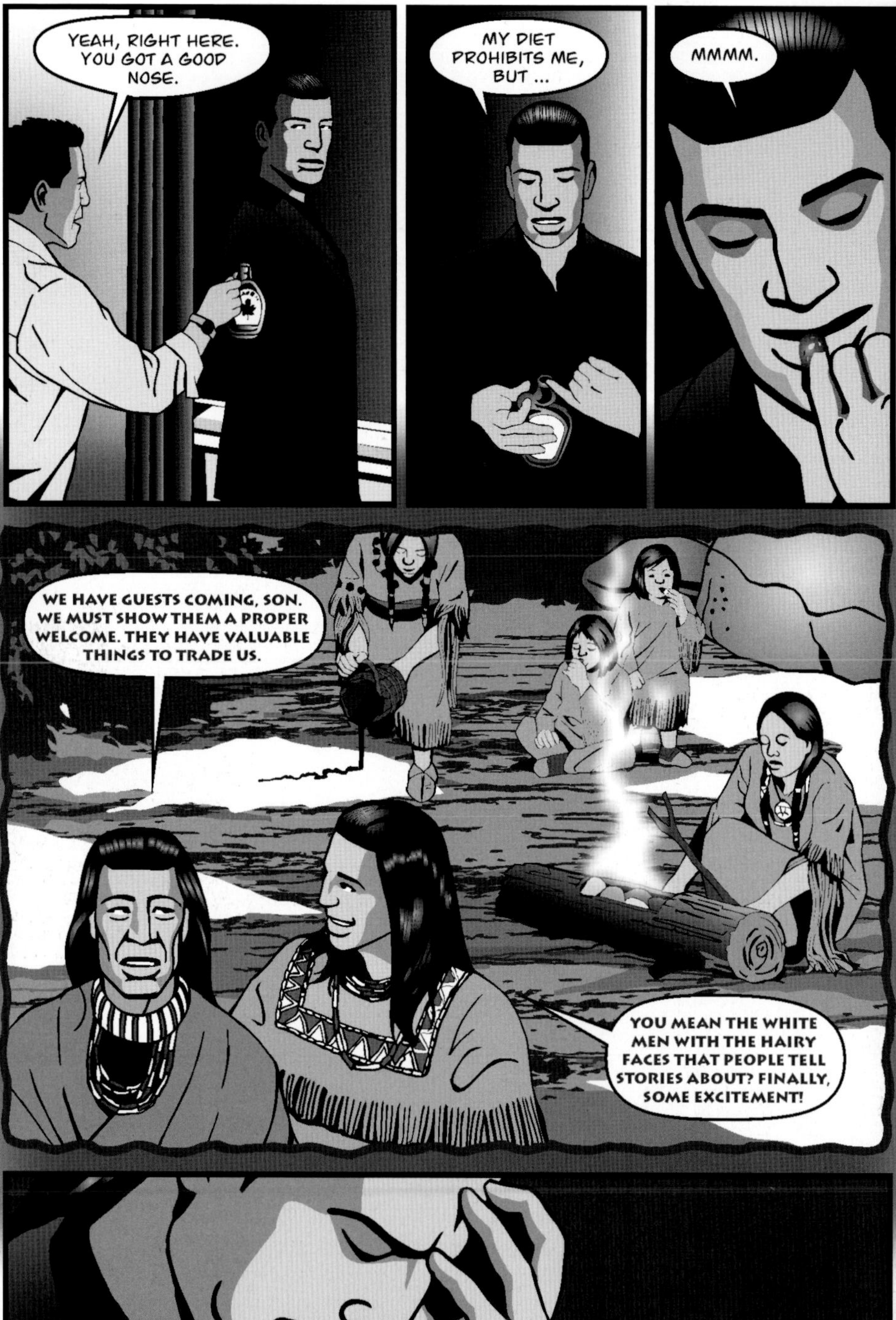
YEAH, RIGHT HERE. YOU GOT A GOOD NOSE.
MY DIET PROHIBITS ME, BUT ...
MMMM.
WE HAVE GUESTS COMING, SON. WE MUST SHOW THEM A PROPER WELCOME. THEY HAVE VALUABLE THINGS TO TRADE US.
YOU MEAN THE WHITE MEN WITH THE HAIRY FACES THAT PEOPLE TELL STORIES ABOUT? FINALLY, SOME EXCITEMENT!

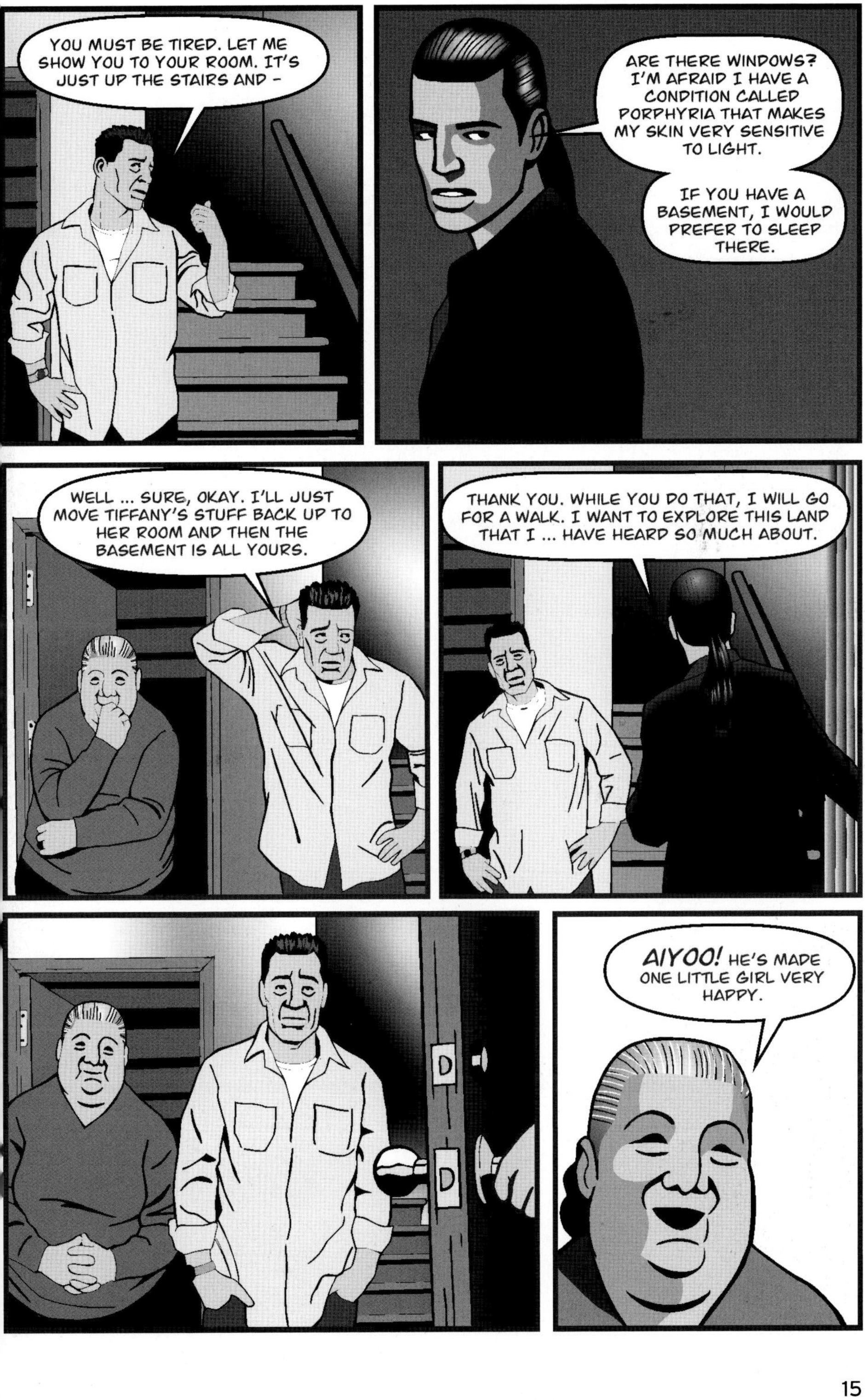
YOU MUST BE TIRED. LET ME SHOW YOU TO YOUR ROOM. IT'S JUST UP THE STAIRS AND –
ARE THERE WINDOWS? I'M AFRAID I HAVE A CONDITION CALLED PORPHYRIA THAT MAKES MY SKIN VERY SENSITIVE TO LIGHT.
IF YOU HAVE A BASEMENT, I WOULD PREFER TO SLEEP THERE.
WELL ... SURE, OKAY. I'LL JUST MOVE TIFFANY'S STUFF BACK UP TO HER ROOM AND THEN THE BASEMENT IS ALL YOURS.
THANK YOU. WHILE YOU DO THAT, I WILL GO FOR A WALK. I WANT TO EXPLORE THIS LAND THAT I ... HAVE HEARD SO MUCH ABOUT.
AIYOO! HE'S MADE ONE LITTLE GIRL VERY HAPPY.

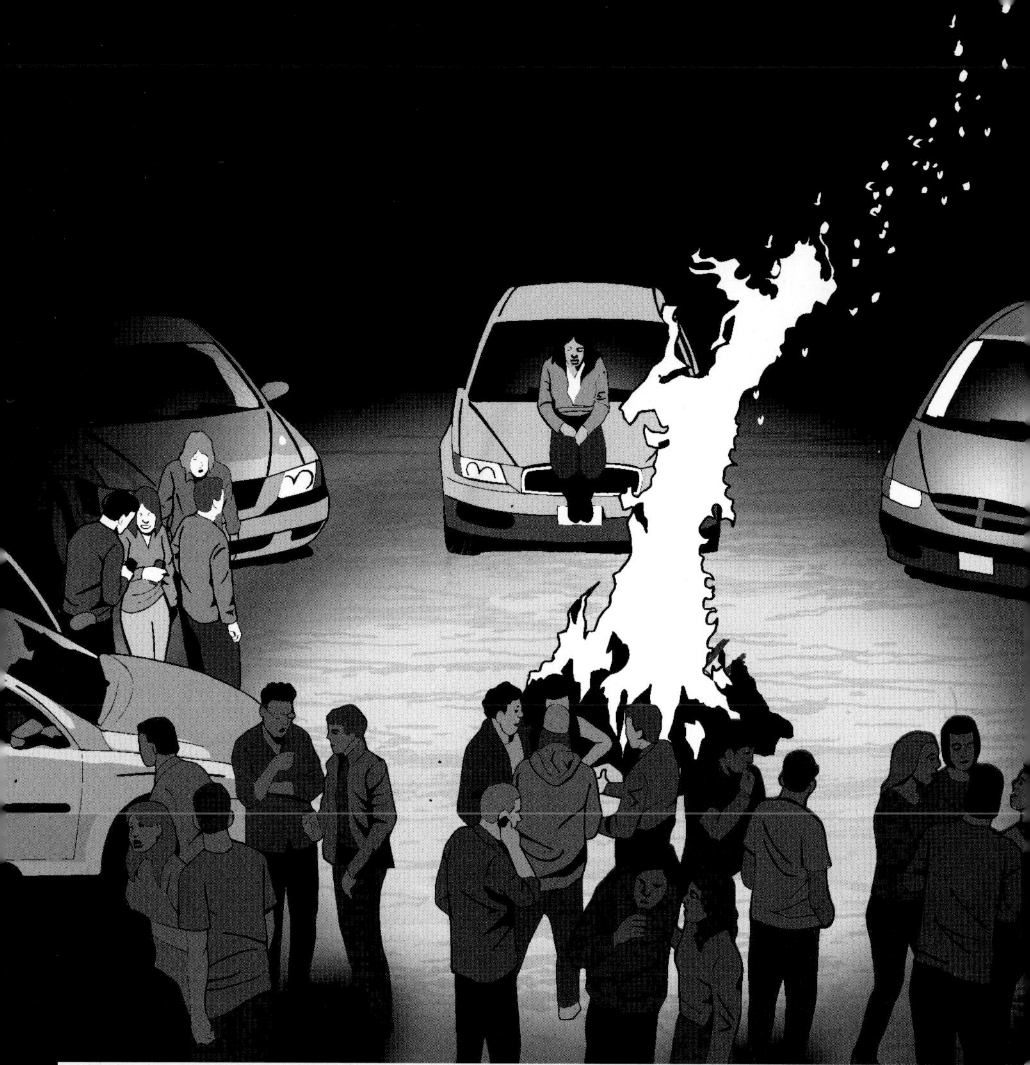

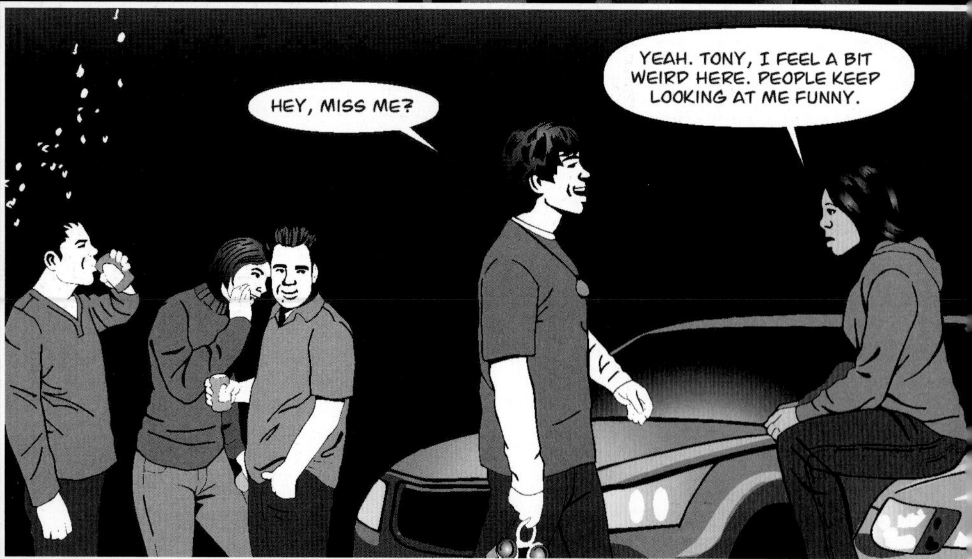
HEY, MISS ME?
YEAH. TONY, I FEEL A BIT WEIRD HERE. PEOPLE KEEP LOOKING AT ME FUNNY.

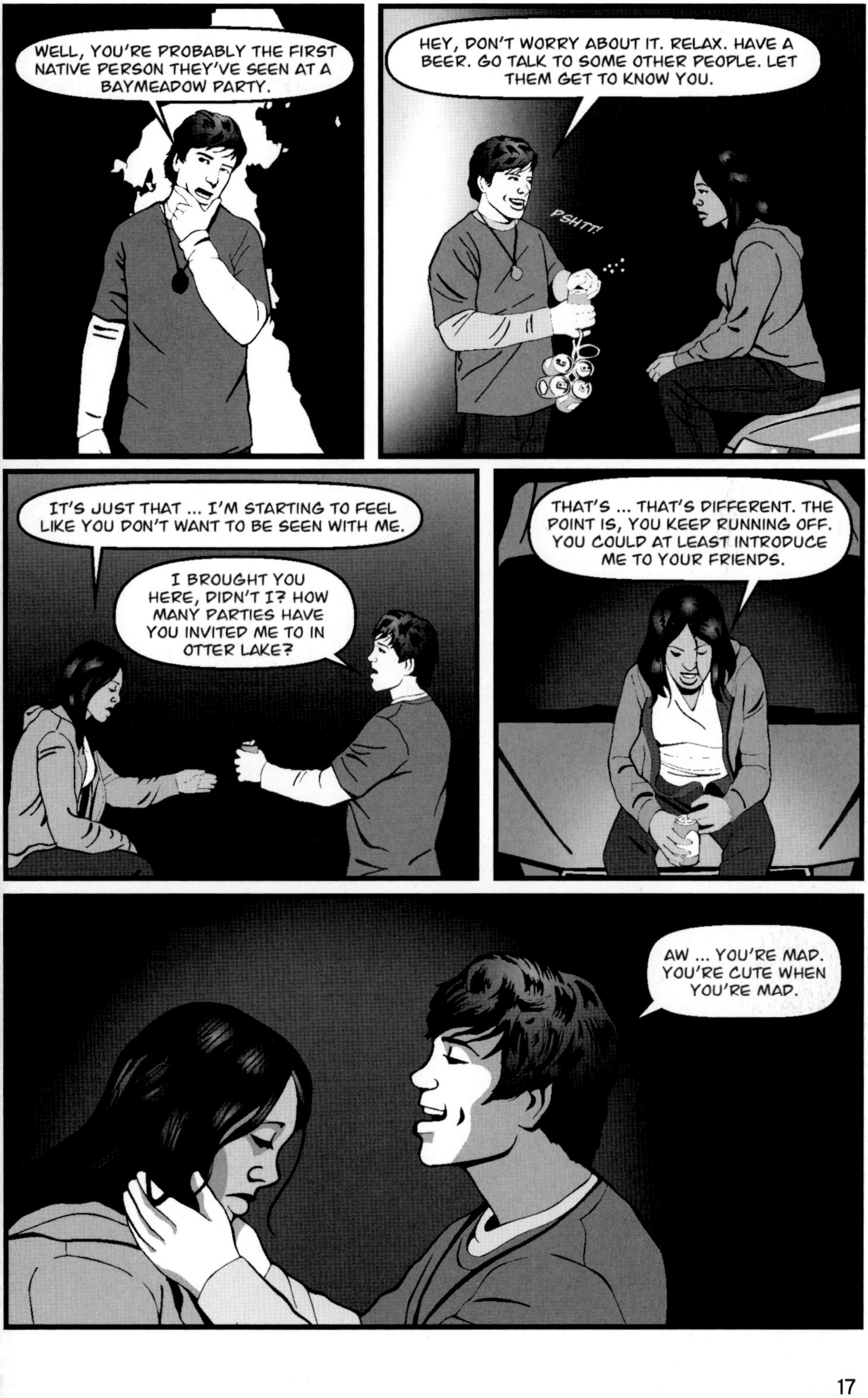
WELL, YOU'RE PROBABLY THE FIRST NATIVE PERSON THEY'VE SEEN AT A BAYMEADOW PARTY.
HEY, DON'T WORRY ABOUT IT. RELAX. HAVE A BEER. GO TALK TO SOME OTHER PEOPLE. LET THEM GET TO KNOW YOU.
PSHTT!
IT'S JUST THAT ... I'M STARTING TO FEEL LIKE YOU DON'T WANT TO BE SEEN WITH ME.
I BROUGHT YOU HERE, DIDN'T I? HOW MANY PARTIES HAVE YOU INVITED ME TO IN OTTER LAKE?
THAT'S ... THAT'S DIFFERENT. THE POINT IS, YOU KEEP RUNNING OFF. YOU COULD AT LEAST INTRODUCE ME TO YOUR FRIENDS.
AW ... YOU'RE MAD. YOU'RE CUTE WHEN YOU'RE MAD.

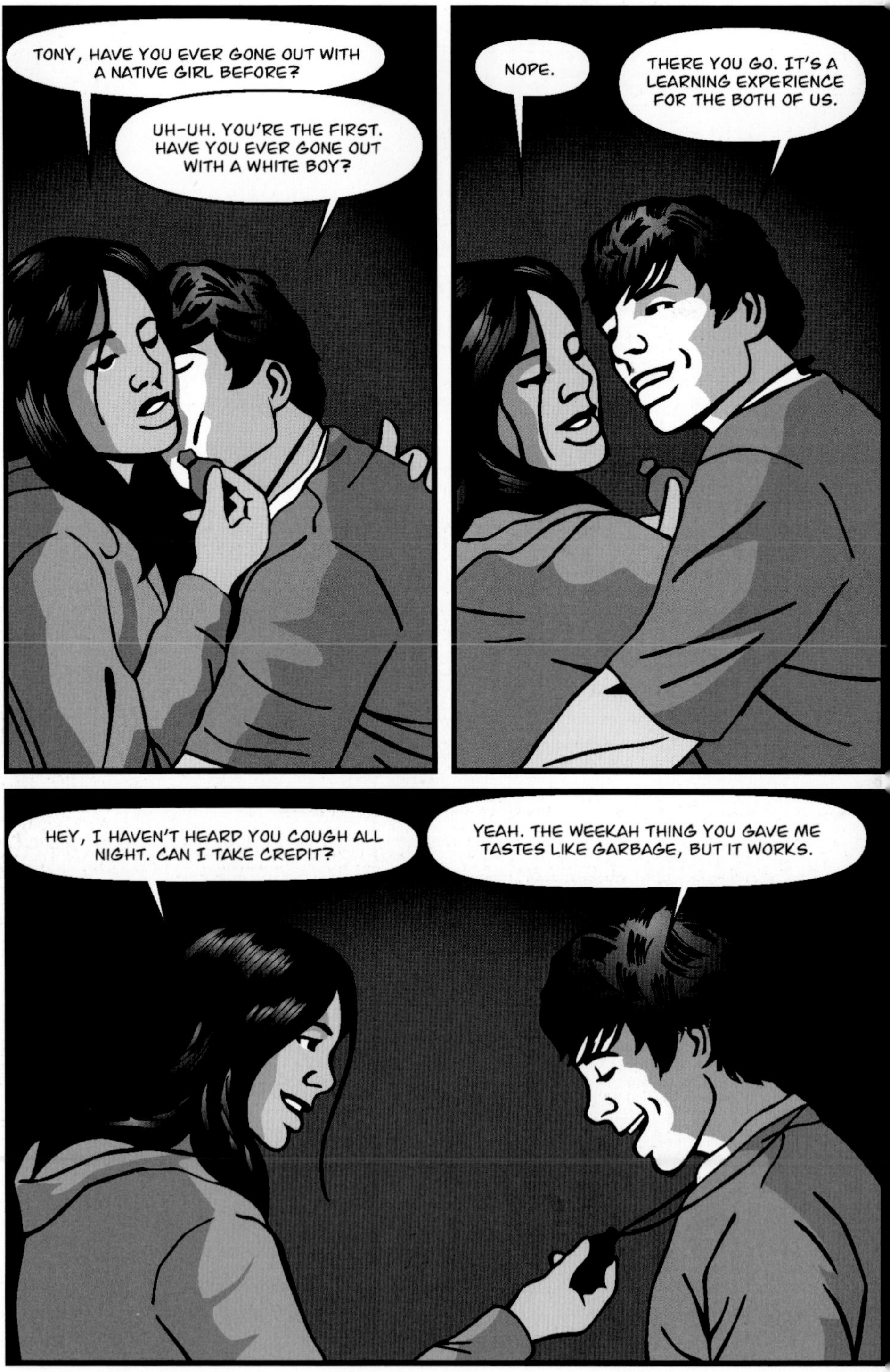
TONY, HAVE YOU EVER GONE OUT WITH A NATIVE GIRL BEFORE?
UH-UH. YOU'RE THE FIRST. HAVE YOU EVER GONE OUT WITH A WHITE BOY?
NOPE.
THERE YOU GO. IT'S A LEARNING EXPERIENCE FOR THE BOTH OF US.
HEY, I HAVEN'T HEARD YOU COUGH ALL NIGHT. CAN I TAKE CREDIT?
YEAH. THE WEEKAH THING YOU GAVE ME TASTES LIKE GARBAGE, BUT IT WORKS.

HEY, TONY! JULIE'S BACK IN TOWN AND SHE WANTS TO SAY HI!
TONY -
JUST A SEC, TIFF! I'LL BE RIGHT BACK.

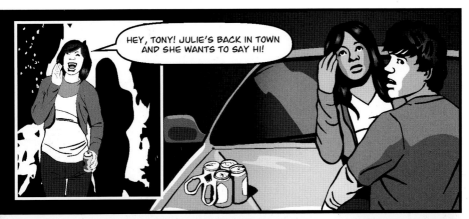

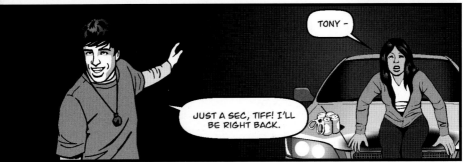

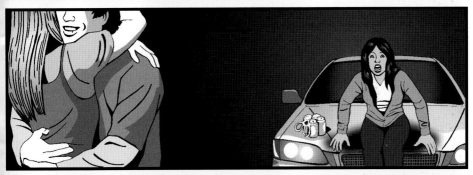

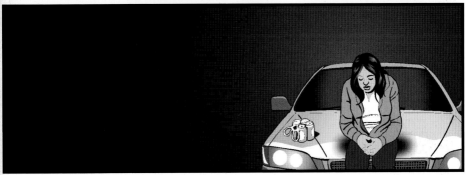

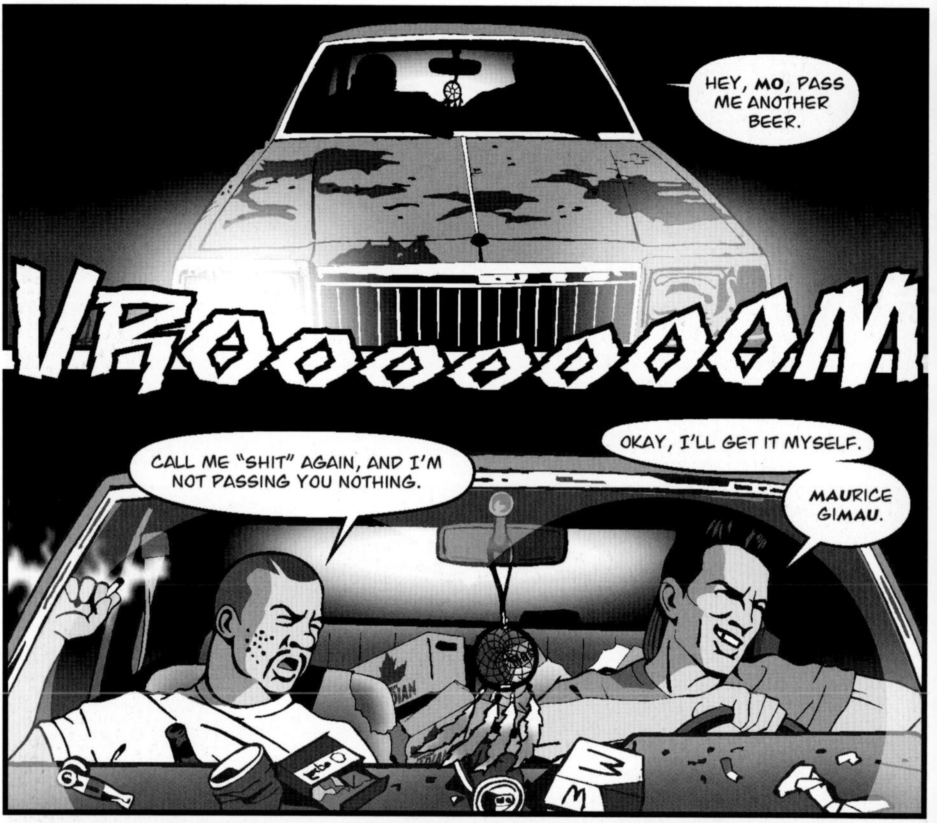
HEY, MO, PASS ME ANOTHER BEER.
VROOOOOOOOM
CALL ME "SHIT" AGAIN, AND I'M NOT PASSING YOU NOTHING.
OKAY, I'LL GET IT MYSELF.
MAURICE GIMAU.

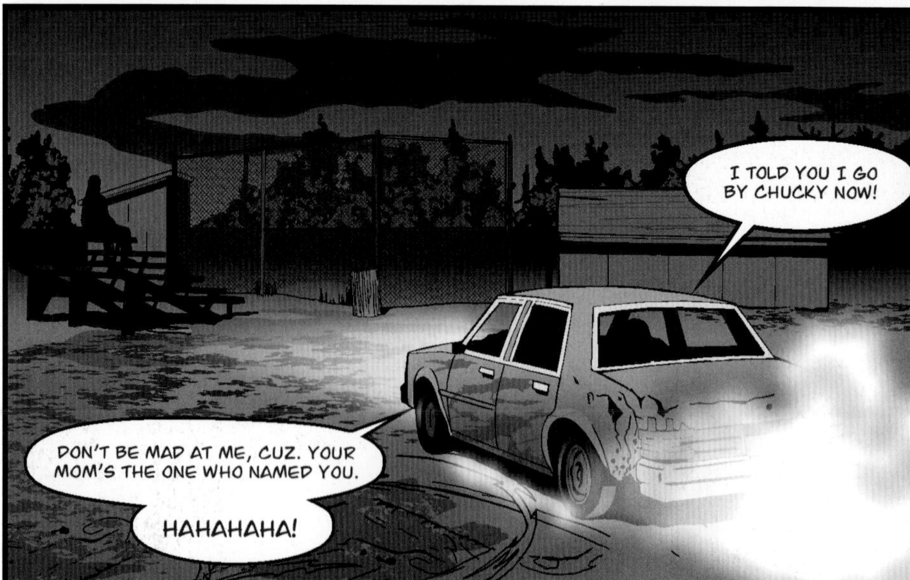
I TOLD YOU I GO BY CHUCKY NOW!
DON'T BE MAD AT ME, CUZ. YOUR MOM'S THE ONE WHO NAMED YOU.
HAHAHAHA!

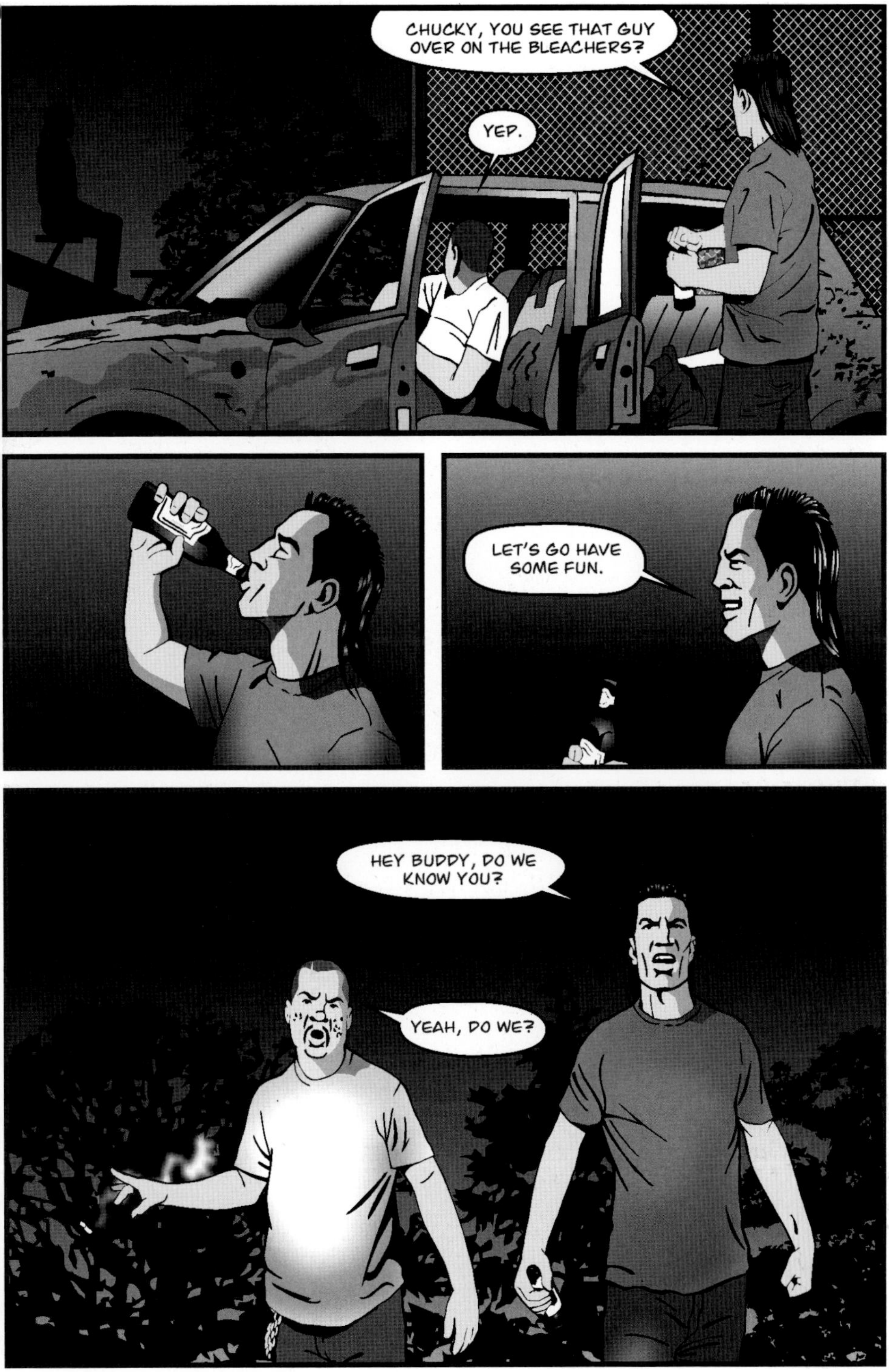
CHUCKY, YOU SEE THAT GUY OVER ON THE BLEACHERS?
YEP.
LET'S GO HAVE SOME FUN.
HEY BUDDY, DO WE KNOW YOU?
YEAH, DO WE?

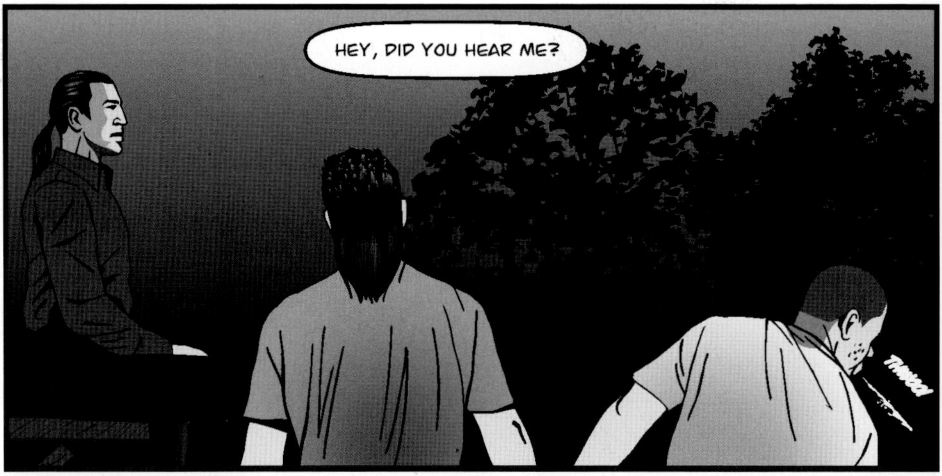

HEY, DID YOU HEAR ME?

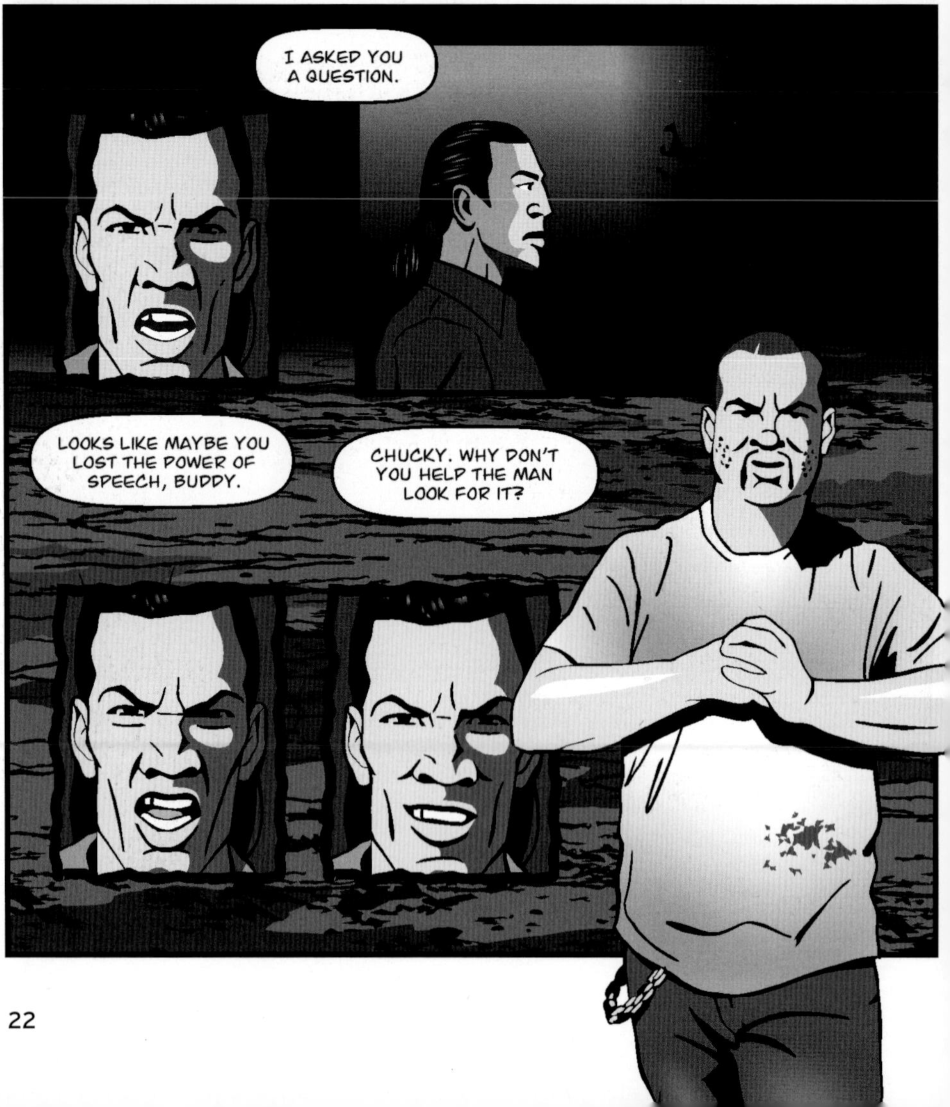

I ASKED YOU A QUESTION.
LOOKS LIKE MAYBE YOU LOST THE POWER OF SPEECH, BUDDY.
CHUCKY. WHY DON'T YOU HELP THE MAN LOOK FOR IT?

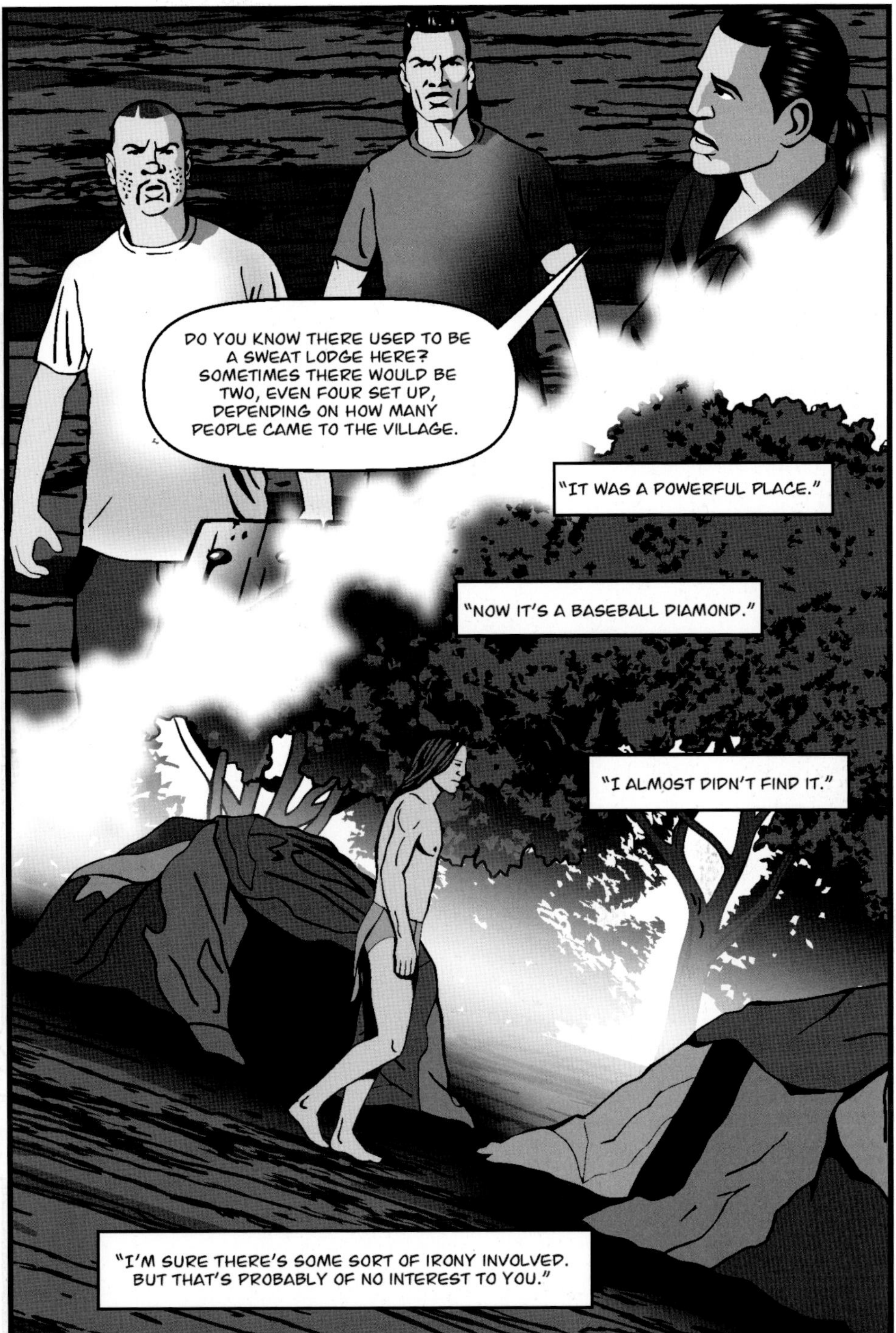
DO YOU KNOW THERE USED TO BE A SWEAT LODGE HERE? SOMETIMES THERE WOULD BE TWO, EVEN FOUR SET UP, DEPENDING ON HOW MANY PEOPLE CAME TO THE VILLAGE.
"IT WAS A POWERFUL PLACE."
"NOW IT'S A BASEBALL DIAMOND."
"I ALMOST DIDN'T FIND IT."
"I'M SURE THERE'S SOME SORT OF IRONY INVOLVED. BUT THAT'S PROBABLY OF NO INTEREST TO YOU."

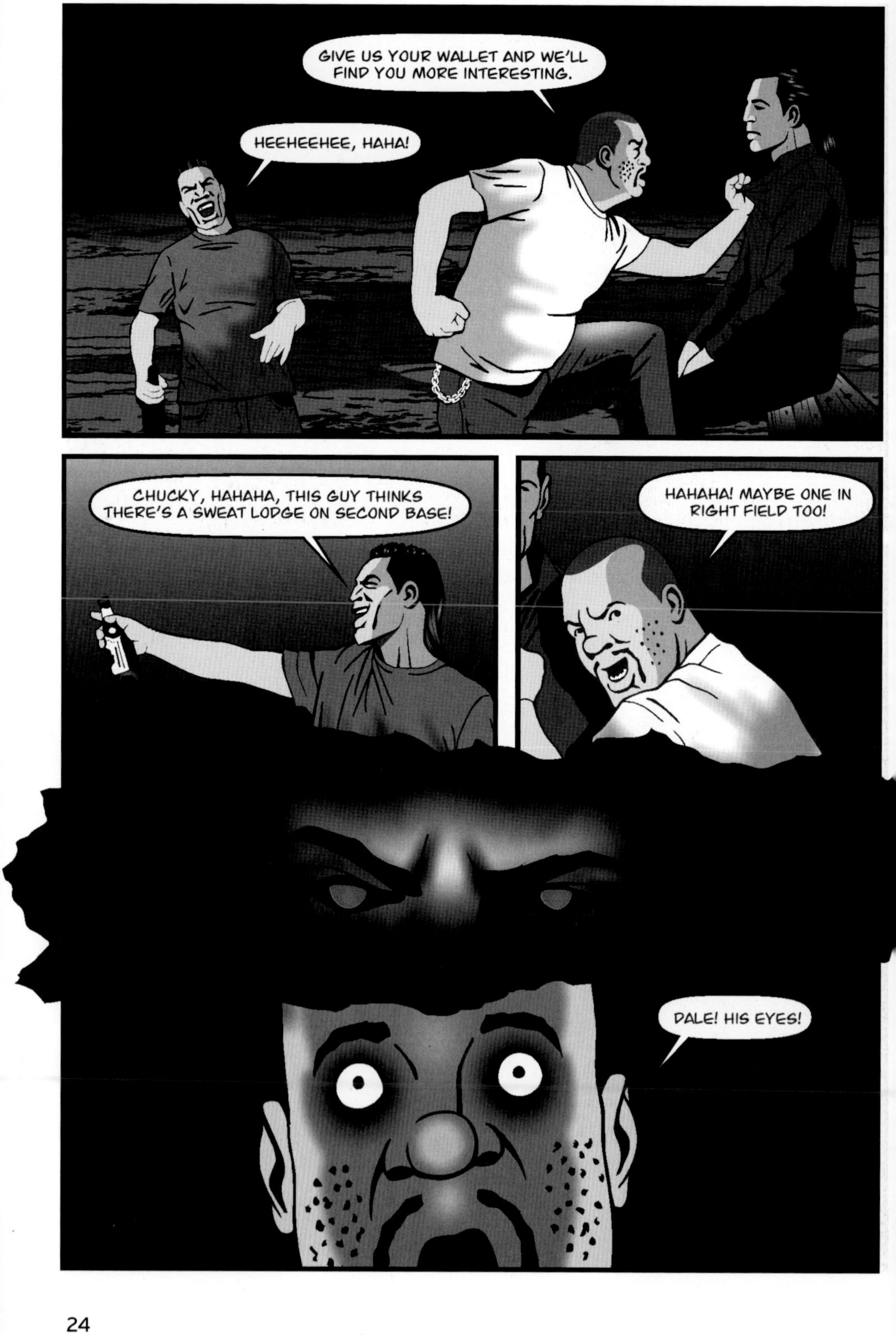
GIVE US YOUR WALLET AND WE'LL FIND YOU MORE INTERESTING.
HEEHEEHEE, HAHA!
CHUCKY, HAHAHA, THIS GUY THINKS THERE'S A SWEAT LODGE ON SECOND BASE!
HAHAHA! MAYBE ONE IN RIGHT FIELD TOO!
DALE! HIS EYES!

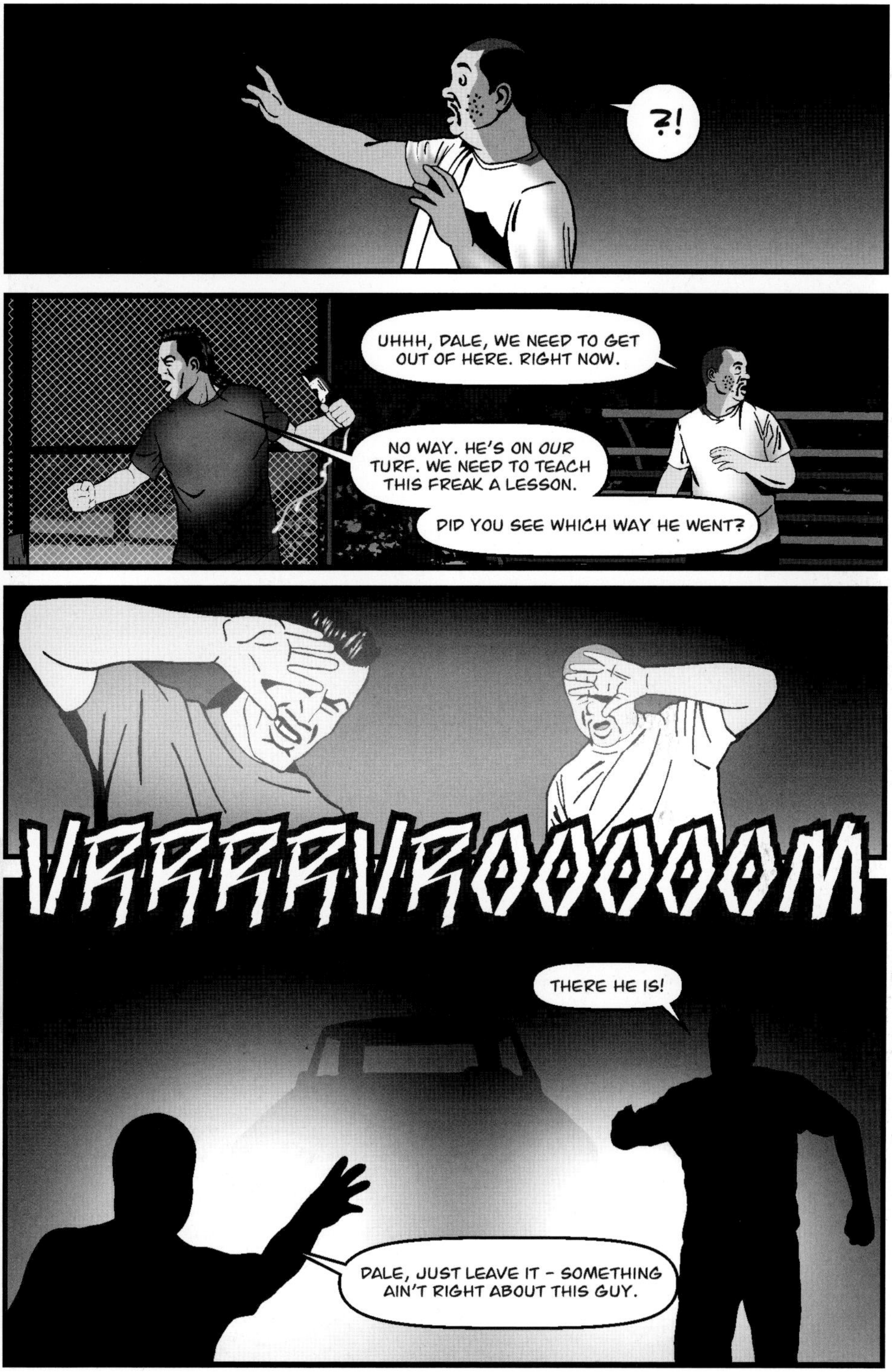
?!
UHHH, DALE, WE NEED TO GET OUT OF HERE. RIGHT NOW.
NO WAY. HE'S ON *OUR* TURF. WE NEED TO TEACH THIS FREAK A LESSON.
DID YOU SEE WHICH WAY HE WENT?
VRRRRVROOOOOM
THERE HE IS!
DALE, JUST LEAVE IT - SOMETHING AIN'T RIGHT ABOUT THIS GUY.

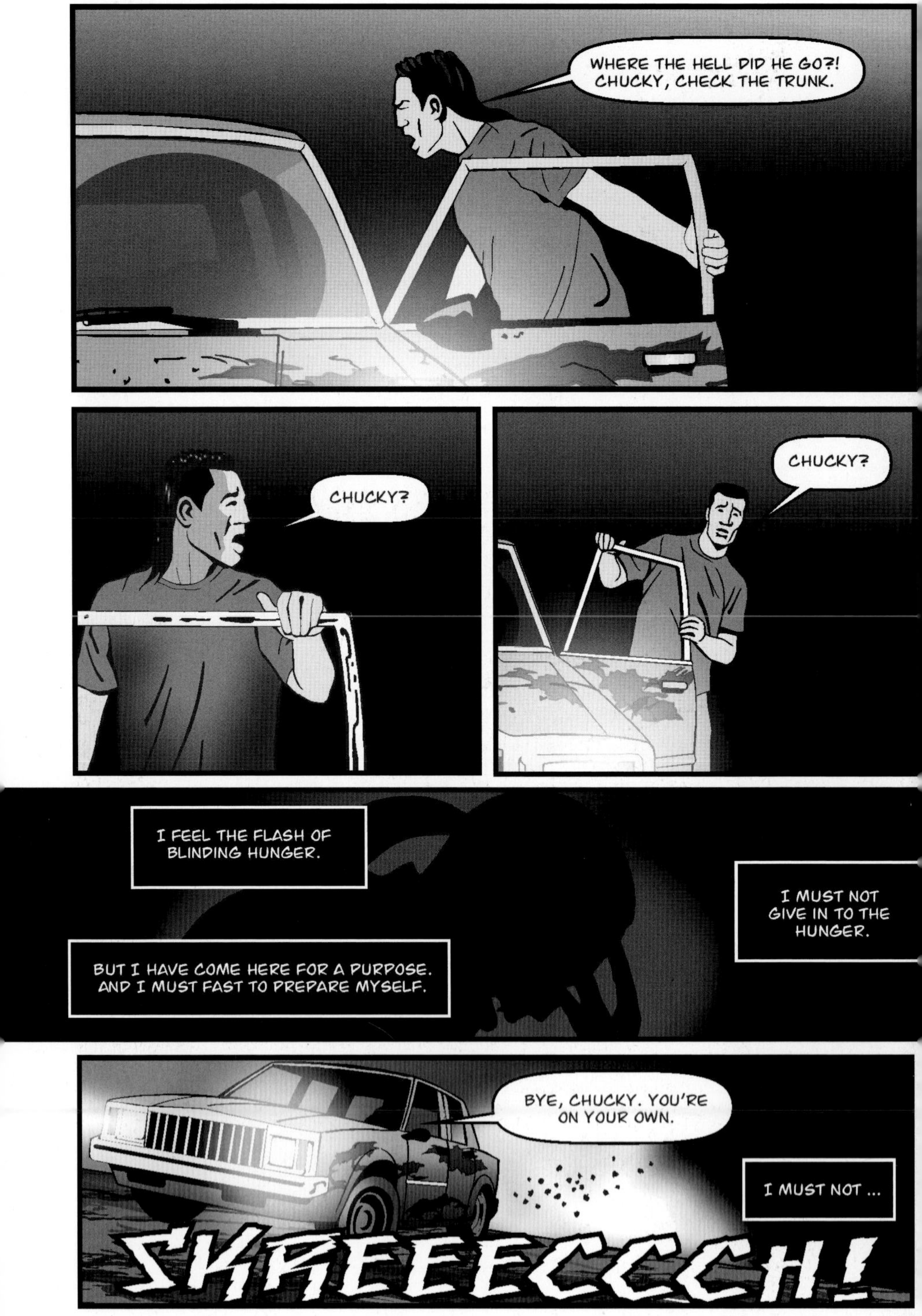
WHERE THE HELL DID HE GO?! CHUCKY, CHECK THE TRUNK.
CHUCKY?
CHUCKY?
I FEEL THE FLASH OF BLINDING HUNGER.
I MUST NOT GIVE IN TO THE HUNGER.
BUT I HAVE COME HERE FOR A PURPOSE. AND I MUST FAST TO PREPARE MYSELF.
BYE, CHUCKY. YOU'RE ON YOUR OWN.
I MUST NOT ...
SKREEECCCH!

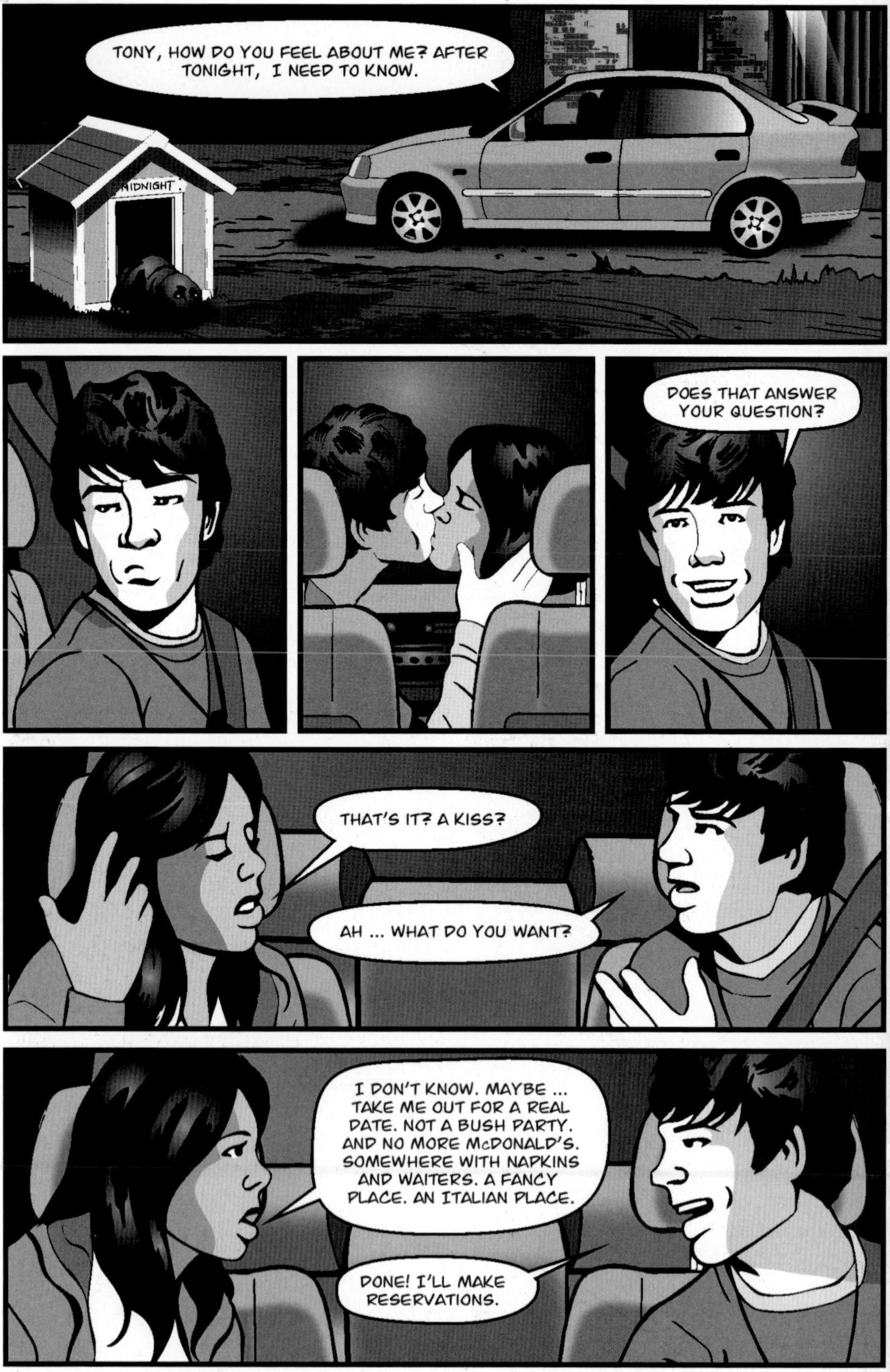
TONY, HOW DO YOU FEEL ABOUT ME? AFTER TONIGHT, I NEED TO KNOW.
MIDNIGHT
DOES THAT ANSWER YOUR QUESTION?
THAT'S IT? A KISS?
AH ... WHAT DO YOU WANT?
I DON'T KNOW. MAYBE ... TAKE ME OUT FOR A REAL DATE. NOT A BUSH PARTY. AND NO MORE McDONALD'S. SOMEWHERE WITH NAPKINS AND WAITERS. A FANCY PLACE. AN ITALIAN PLACE.
DONE! I'LL MAKE RESERVATIONS.

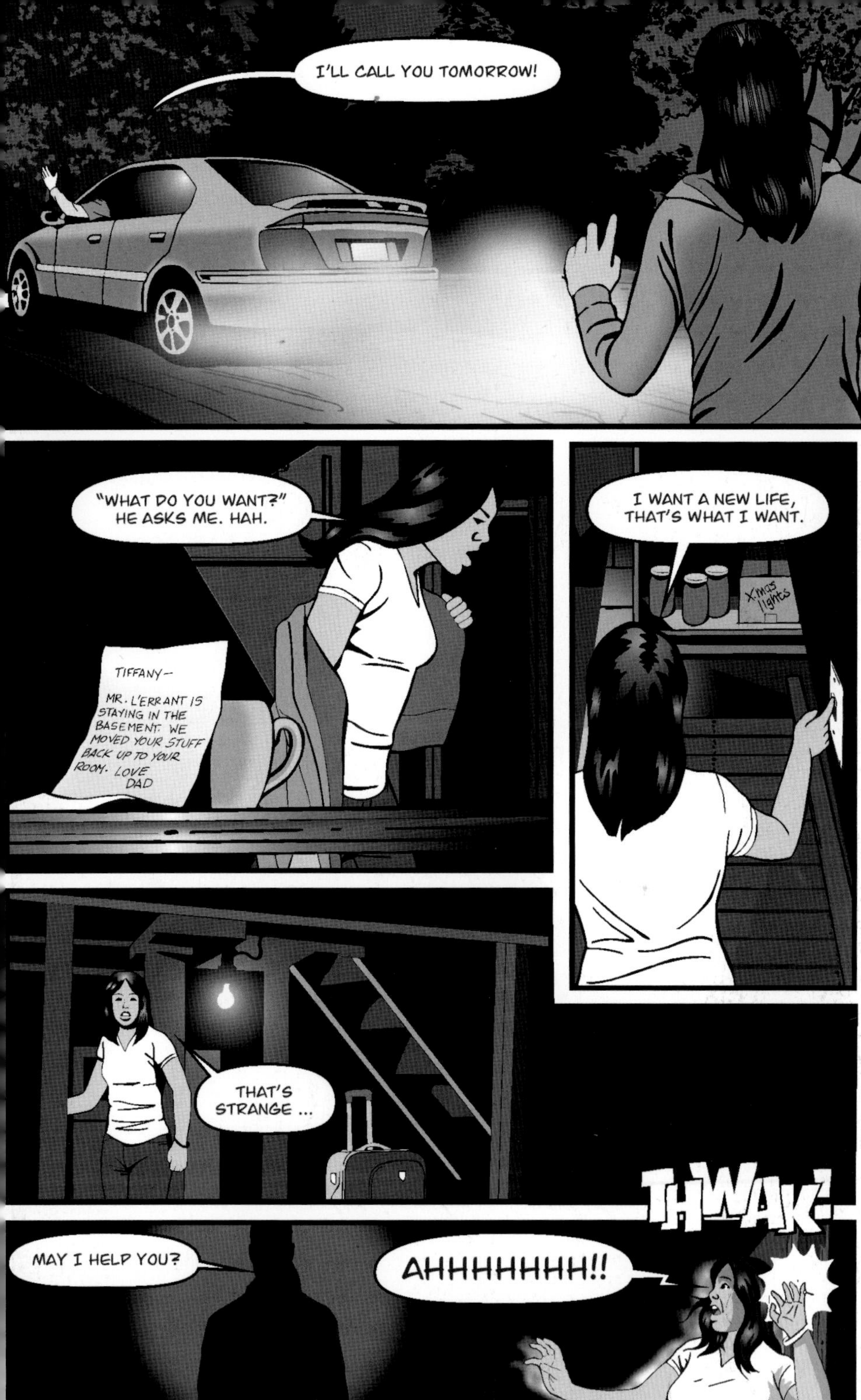
I'LL CALL YOU TOMORROW!
"WHAT DO YOU WANT?" HE ASKS ME. HAH.
TIFFANY— MR. L'ERRANT IS STAYING IN THE BASEMENT. WE MOVED YOUR STUFF BACK UP TO YOUR ROOM. LOVE DAD
I WANT A NEW LIFE, THAT'S WHAT I WANT.
X-mas lights
THAT'S STRANGE ...
THWAK!
MAY I HELP YOU?
AHHHHHHH!!

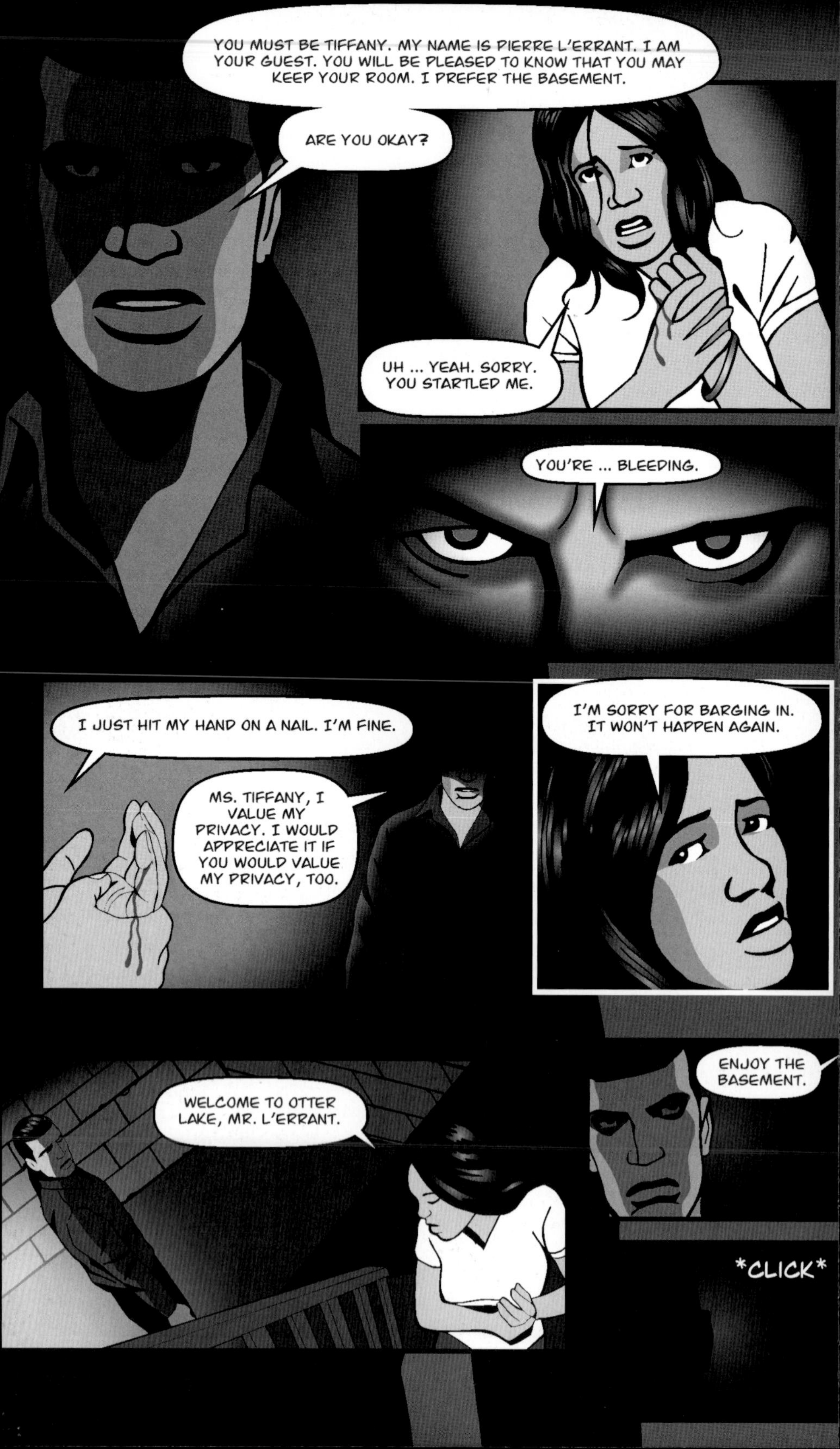
YOU MUST BE TIFFANY. MY NAME IS PIERRE L'ERRANT. I AM YOUR GUEST. YOU WILL BE PLEASED TO KNOW THAT YOU MAY KEEP YOUR ROOM. I PREFER THE BASEMENT.
ARE YOU OKAY?
UH ... YEAH. SORRY. YOU STARTLED ME.
YOU'RE ... BLEEDING.
I JUST HIT MY HAND ON A NAIL. I'M FINE.
MS. TIFFANY, I VALUE MY PRIVACY. I WOULD APPRECIATE IT IF YOU WOULD VALUE MY PRIVACY, TOO.
I'M SORRY FOR BARGING IN. IT WON'T HAPPEN AGAIN.
WELCOME TO OTTER LAKE, MR. L'ERRANT.
ENJOY THE BASEMENT.
CLICK

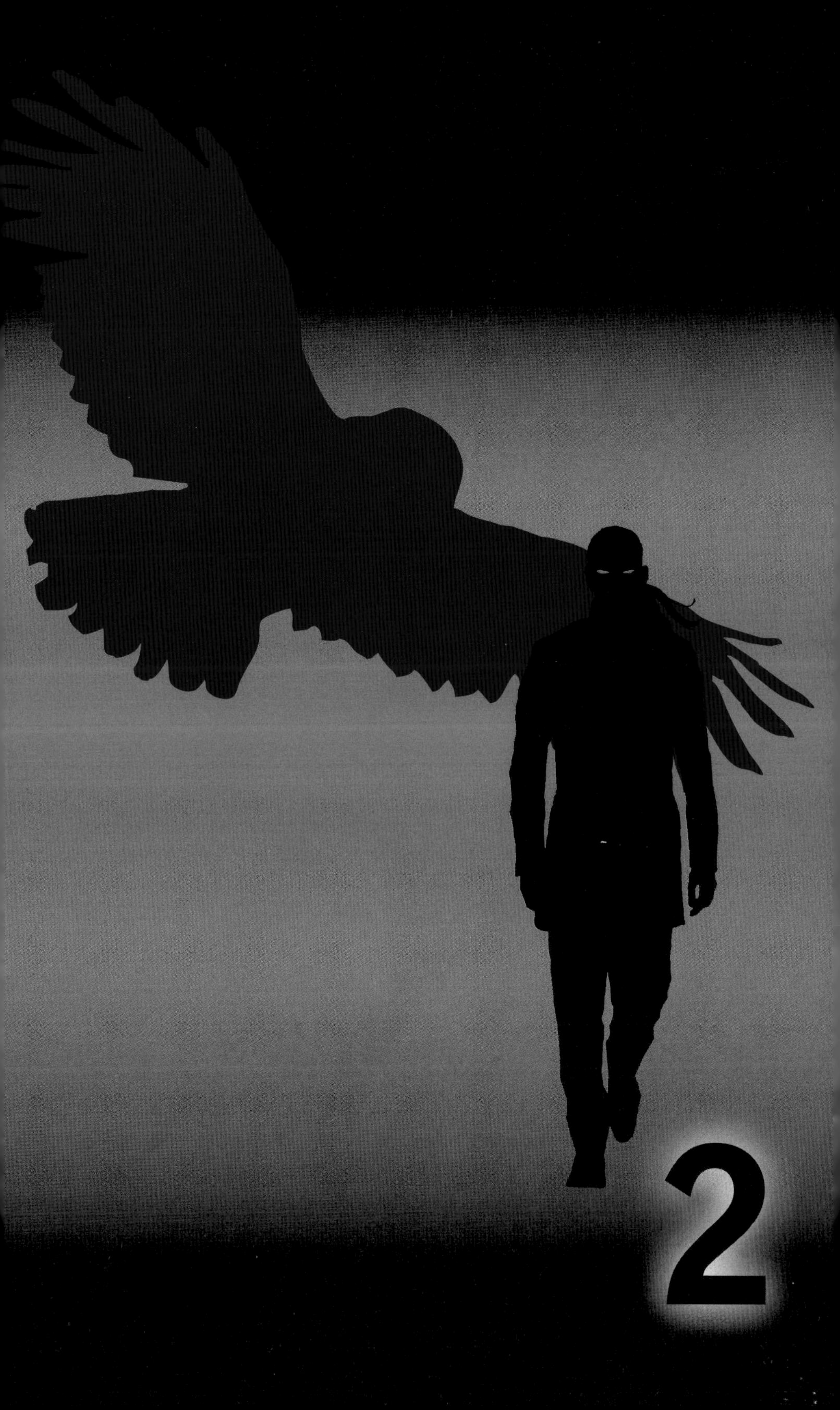
2

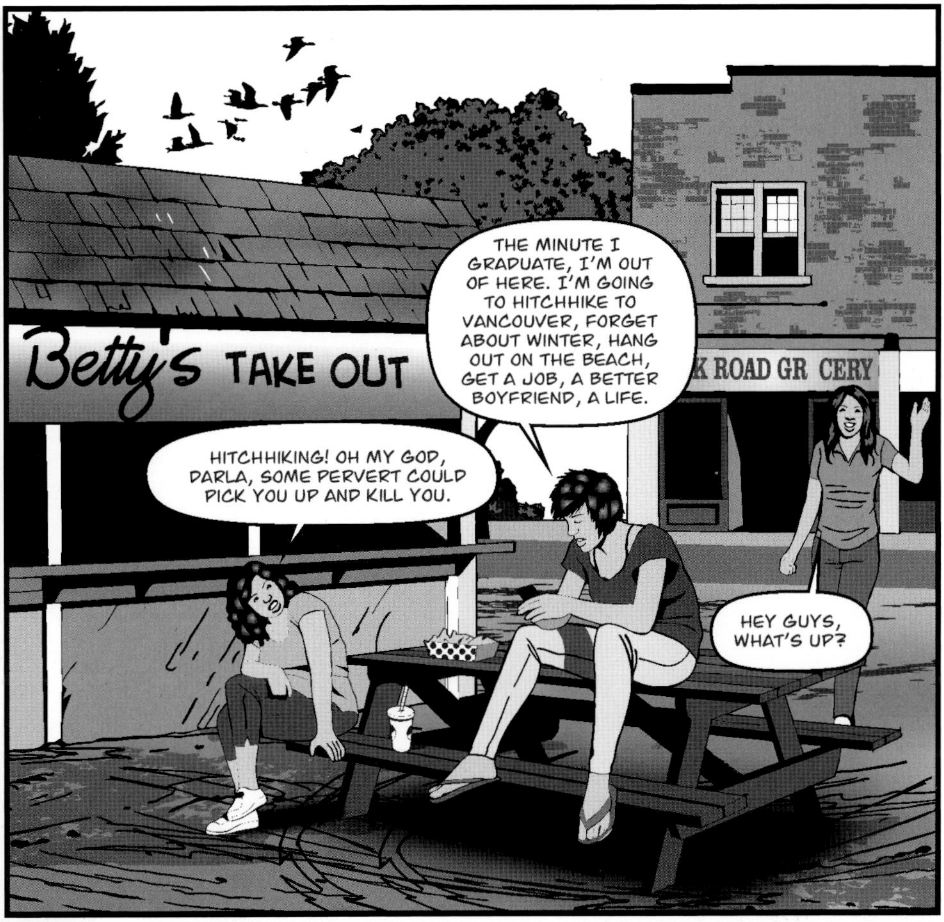
Betty's TAKE OUT
K ROAD GR CERY
THE MINUTE I GRADUATE, I'M OUT OF HERE. I'M GOING TO HITCHHIKE TO VANCOUVER, FORGET ABOUT WINTER, HANG OUT ON THE BEACH, GET A JOB, A BETTER BOYFRIEND, A LIFE.
HITCHHIKING! OH MY GOD, DARLA, SOME PERVERT COULD PICK YOU UP AND KILL YOU.
HEY GUYS, WHAT'S UP?

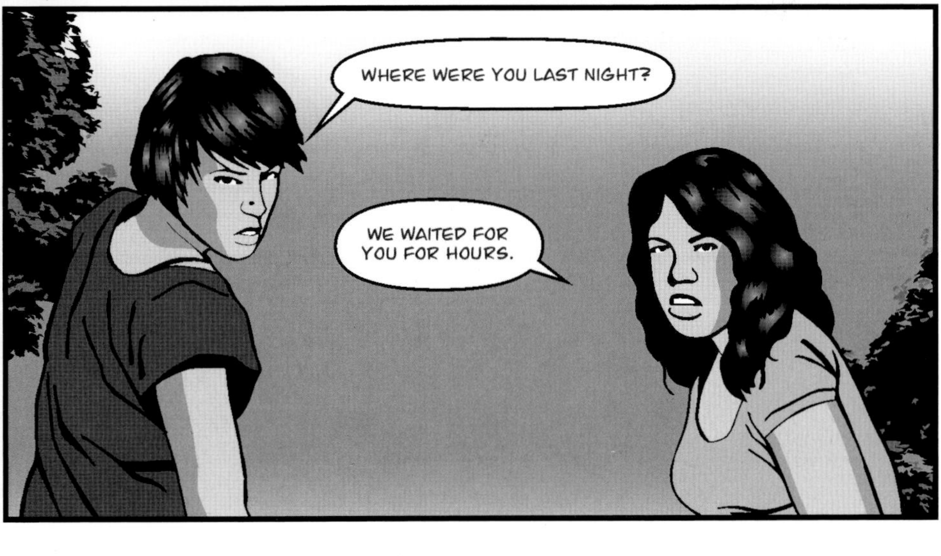
WHERE WERE YOU LAST NIGHT?
WE WAITED FOR YOU FOR HOURS.

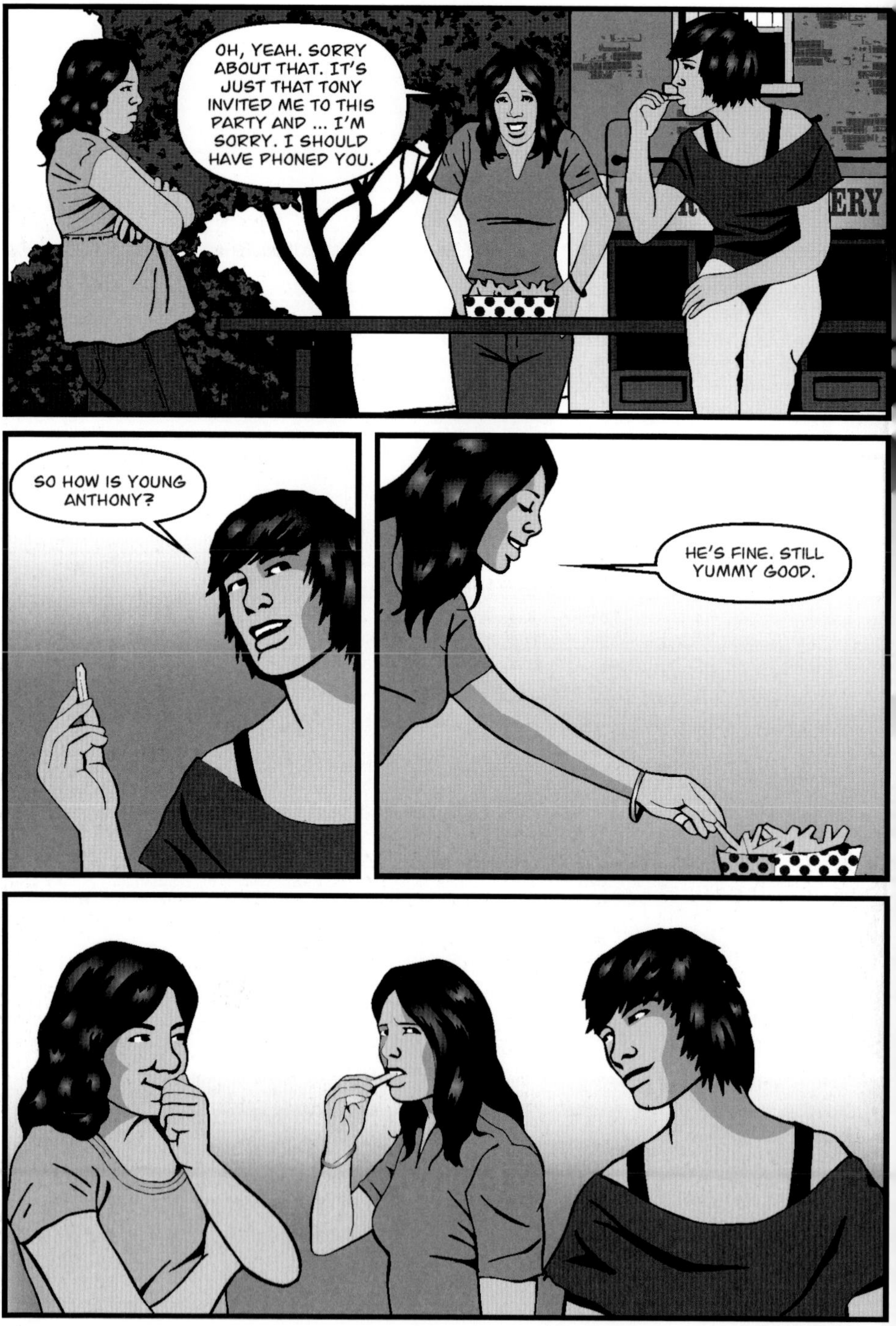
OH, YEAH. SORRY ABOUT THAT. IT'S JUST THAT TONY INVITED ME TO THIS PARTY AND ... I'M SORRY. I SHOULD HAVE PHONED YOU.
SO HOW IS YOUNG ANTHONY?
HE'S FINE. STILL YUMMY GOOD.

WAS JULIE BANES AT THE PARTY TOO?
YEAH. WHY?
WE HEARD SHE'S GOT A BRACELET JUST LIKE YOURS. ONLY HERS IS SOLID GOLD.
DIDN'T YOU TELL US TONY BOUGHT A MATCHING BRACELET AS A BIRTHDAY PRESENT FOR HIS MOM?
YOU HAVE TO ADMIT THAT'S PRETTY WEIRD.
I HEARD TONY AND JULIE USED TO DATE WHEN THEY WERE IN GRADE EIGHT, BUT HER DAD MADE THEM BREAK UP BECAUSE THEY WERE TOO YOUNG.
I HAVE TO GO.
BIG SURPRISE. SHE'S DITCHING US AGAIN.

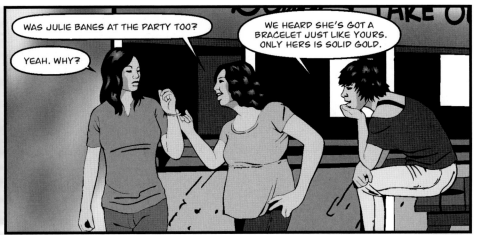

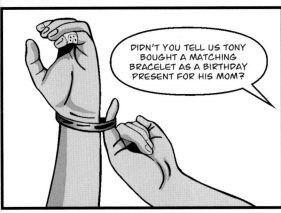

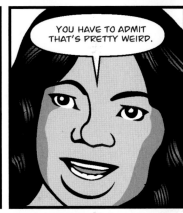

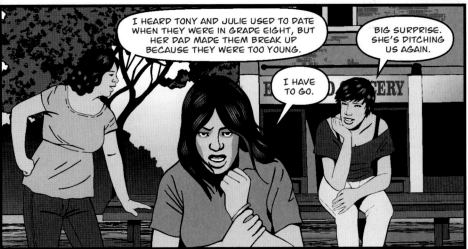

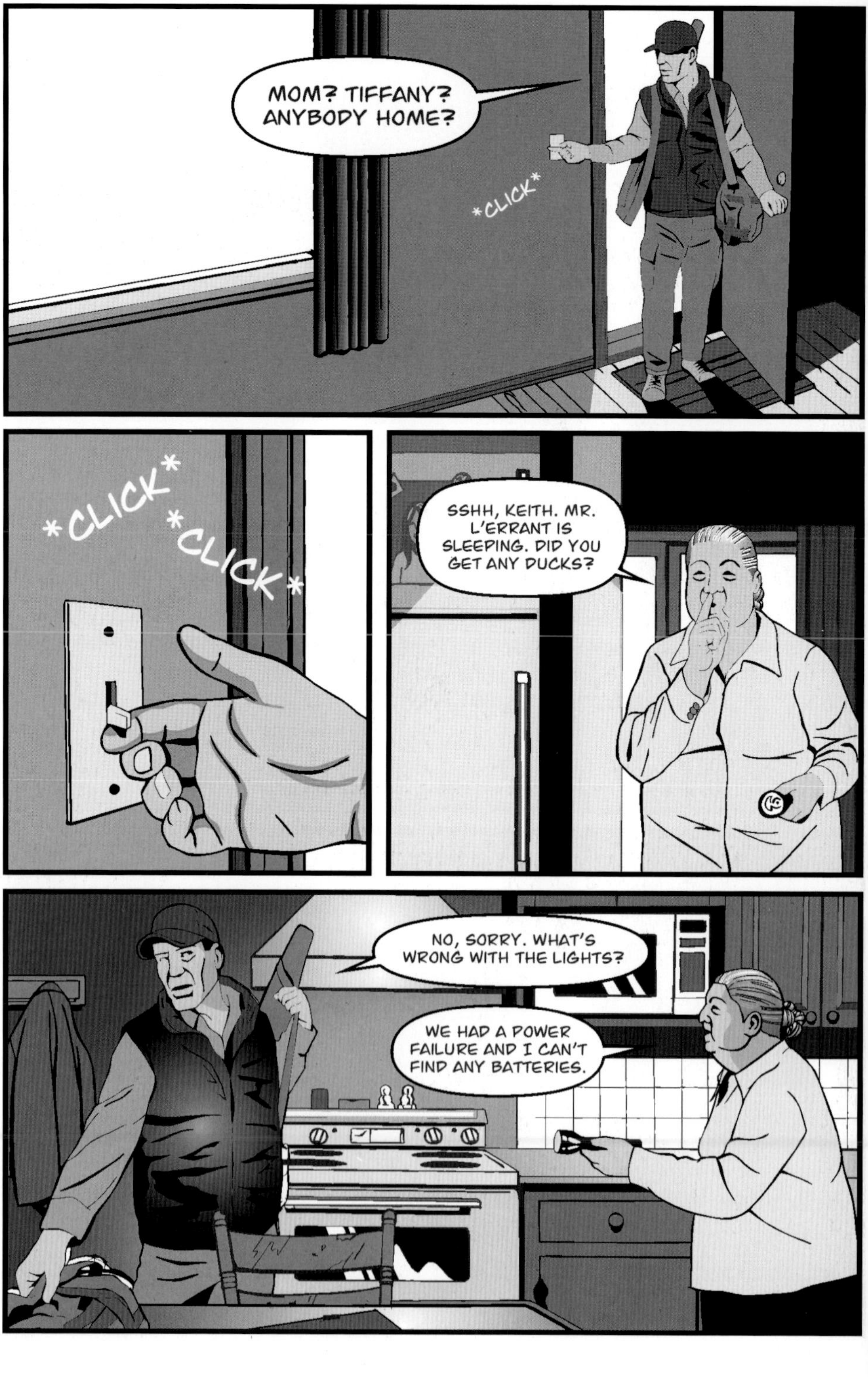
MOM? TIFFANY? ANYBODY HOME?
CLICK
CLICK
CLICK
SSHH, KEITH. MR. L'ERRANT IS SLEEPING. DID YOU GET ANY DUCKS?
NO, SORRY. WHAT'S WRONG WITH THE LIGHTS?
WE HAD A POWER FAILURE AND I CAN'T FIND ANY BATTERIES.

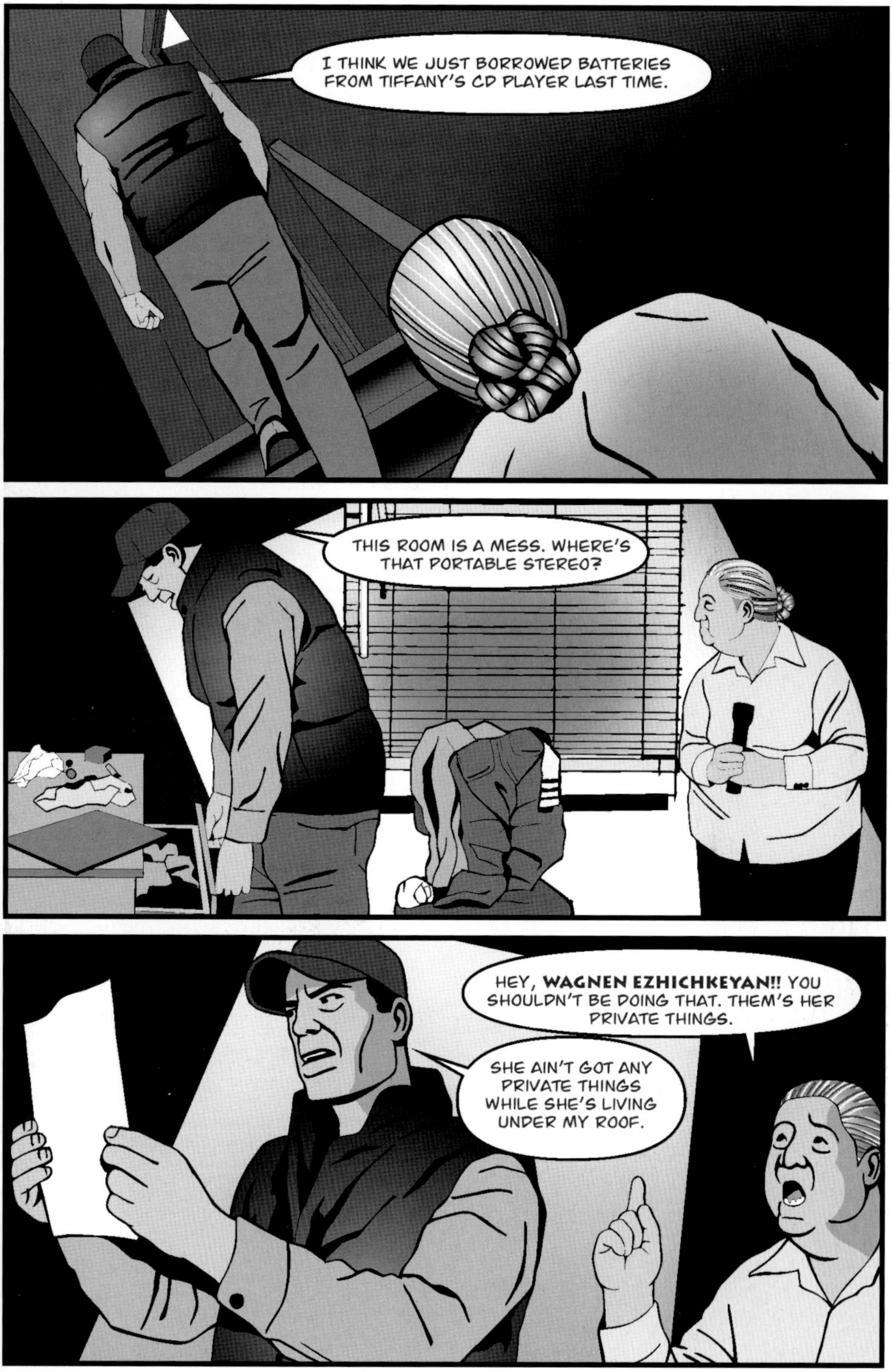
I THINK WE JUST BORROWED BATTERIES FROM TIFFANY'S CD PLAYER LAST TIME.
THIS ROOM IS A MESS. WHERE'S THAT PORTABLE STEREO?
HEY, **WAGNEN EZHICHKEYAN!!** YOU SHOULDN'T BE DOING THAT. THEM'S HER PRIVATE THINGS.
SHE AIN'T GOT ANY PRIVATE THINGS WHILE SHE'S LIVING UNDER MY ROOF.

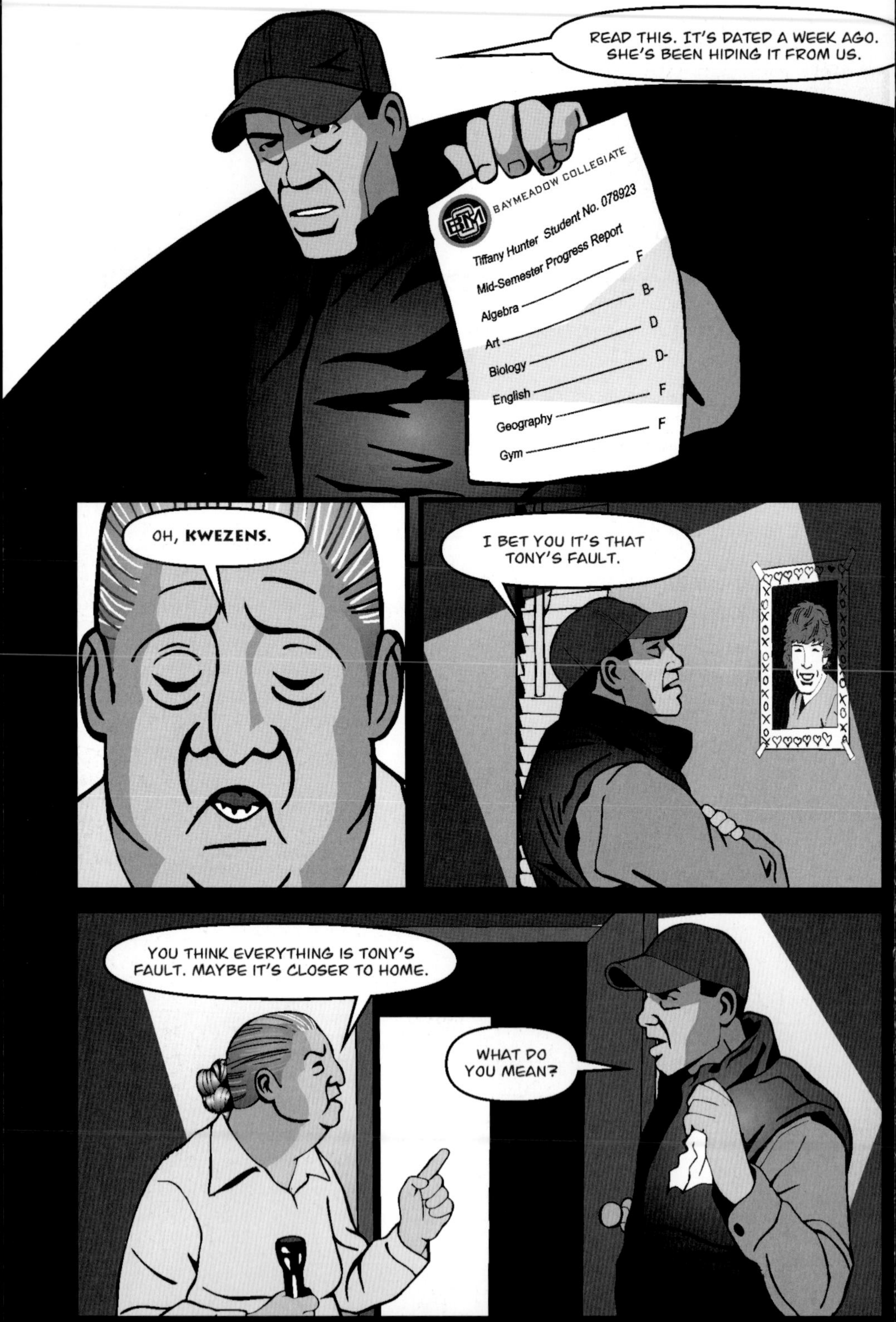
READ THIS. IT'S DATED A WEEK AGO. SHE'S BEEN HIDING IT FROM US.
BAYMEADOW COLLEGIATE
Tiffany Hunter Student No. 078923
Mid-Semester Progress Report
Algebra F
Art B-
Biology D
English D-
Geography F
Gym F
OH, KWEZENS.
I BET YOU IT'S THAT TONY'S FAULT.
YOU THINK EVERYTHING IS TONY'S FAULT. MAYBE IT'S CLOSER TO HOME.
WHAT DO YOU MEAN?

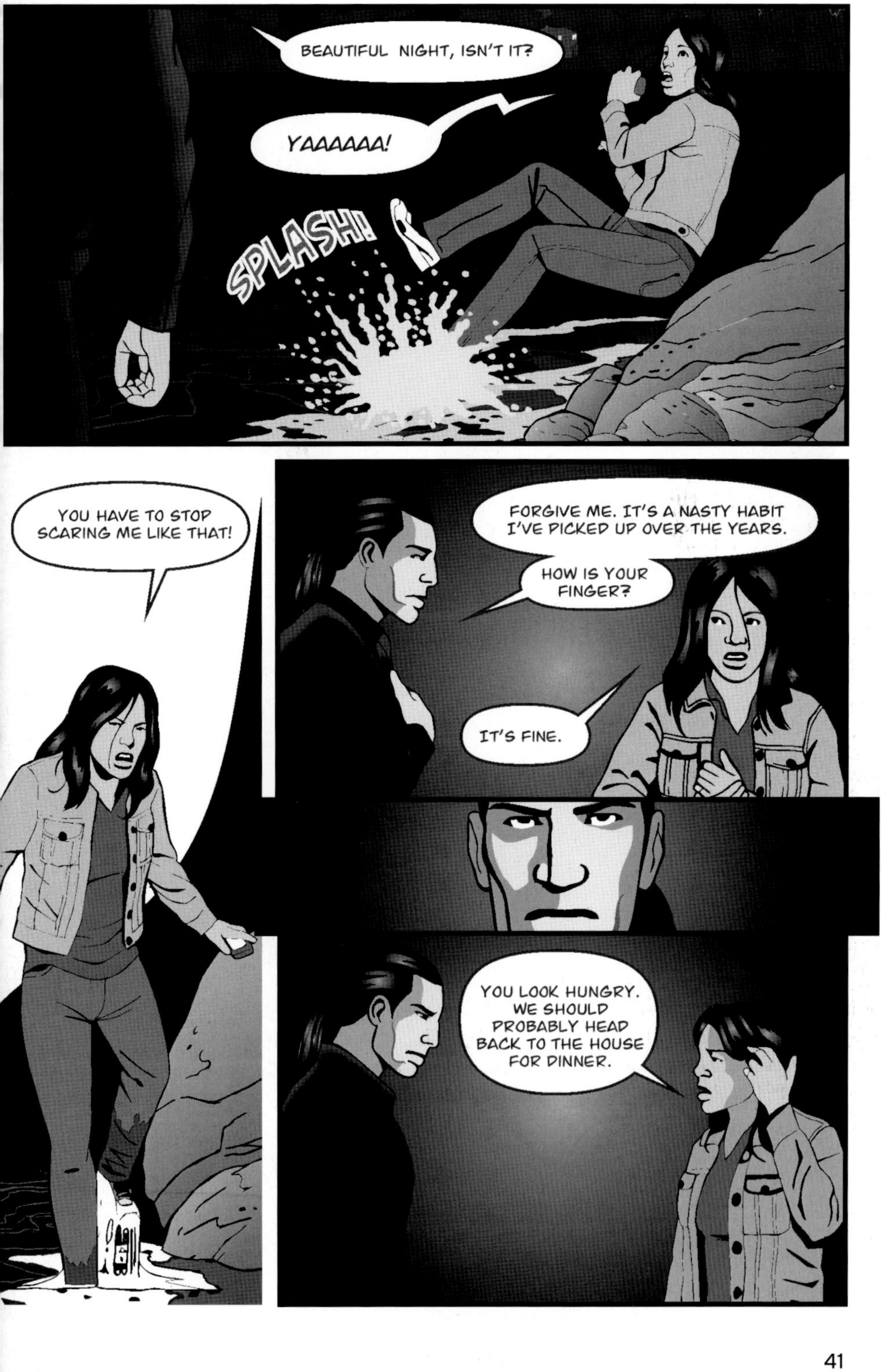
BEAUTIFUL NIGHT, ISN'T IT?
YAAAAAA!
SPLASH!
YOU HAVE TO STOP SCARING ME LIKE THAT!
FORGIVE ME. IT'S A NASTY HABIT I'VE PICKED UP OVER THE YEARS.
HOW IS YOUR FINGER?
IT'S FINE.
YOU LOOK HUNGRY. WE SHOULD PROBABLY HEAD BACK TO THE HOUSE FOR DINNER.

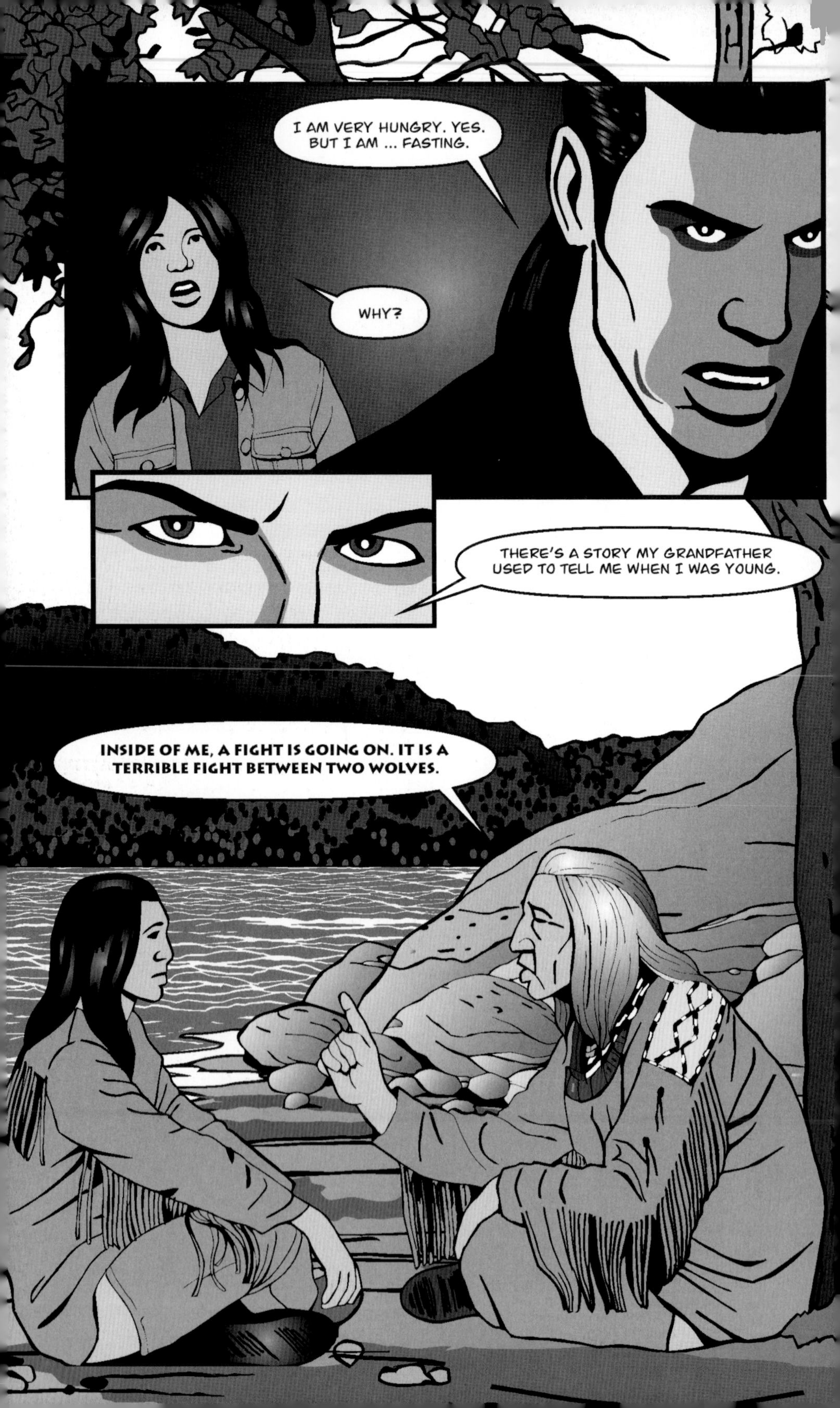
I AM VERY HUNGRY. YES. BUT I AM ... FASTING.
WHY?
THERE'S A STORY MY GRANDFATHER USED TO TELL ME WHEN I WAS YOUNG.
INSIDE OF ME, A FIGHT IS GOING ON. IT IS A TERRIBLE FIGHT BETWEEN TWO WOLVES.

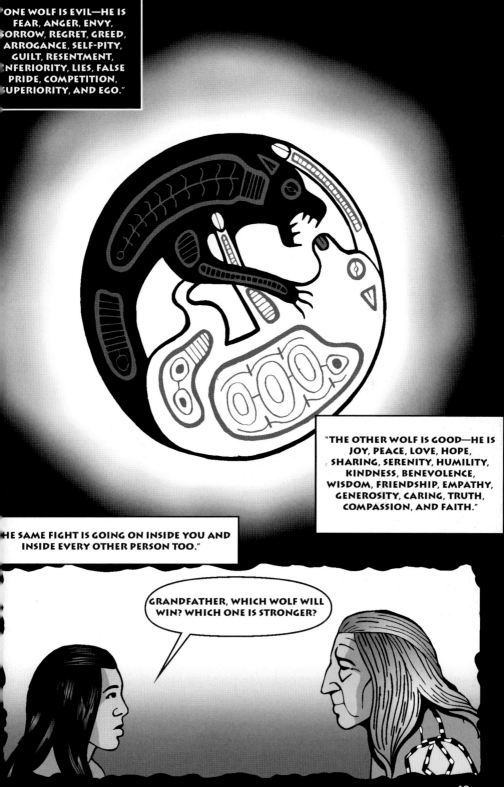

43

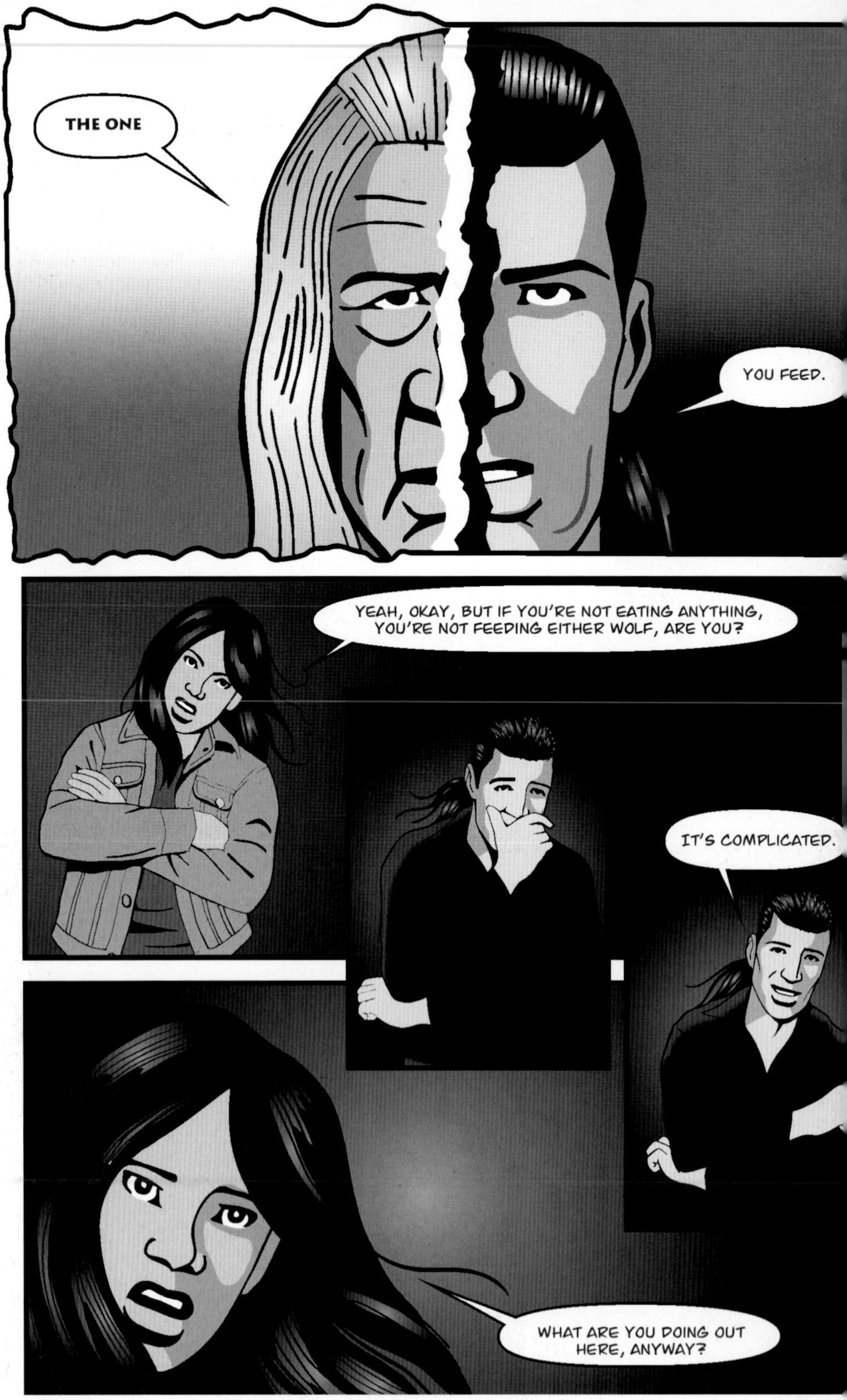
THE ONE
YOU FEED.
YEAH, OKAY, BUT IF YOU'RE NOT EATING ANYTHING, YOU'RE NOT FEEDING EITHER WOLF, ARE YOU?
IT'S COMPLICATED.
WHAT ARE YOU DOING OUT HERE, ANYWAY?

RRRRINGGG
*RRRRINGGG

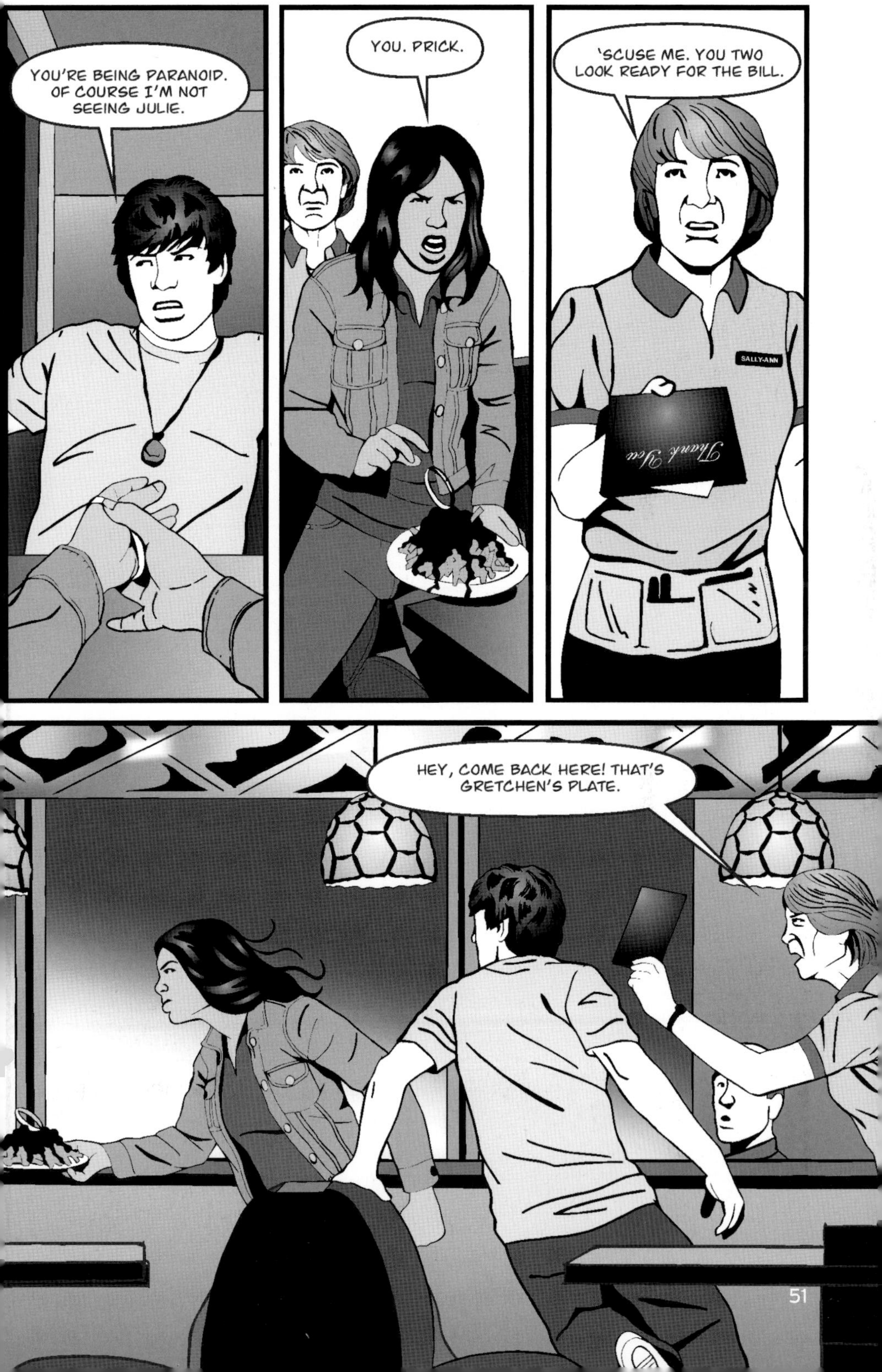
YOU'RE BEING PARANOID. OF COURSE I'M NOT SEEING JULIE.
YOU. PRICK.
'SCUSE ME. YOU TWO LOOK READY FOR THE BILL.
SALLY-ANN
Thank You
HEY, COME BACK HERE! THAT'S GRETCHEN'S PLATE.

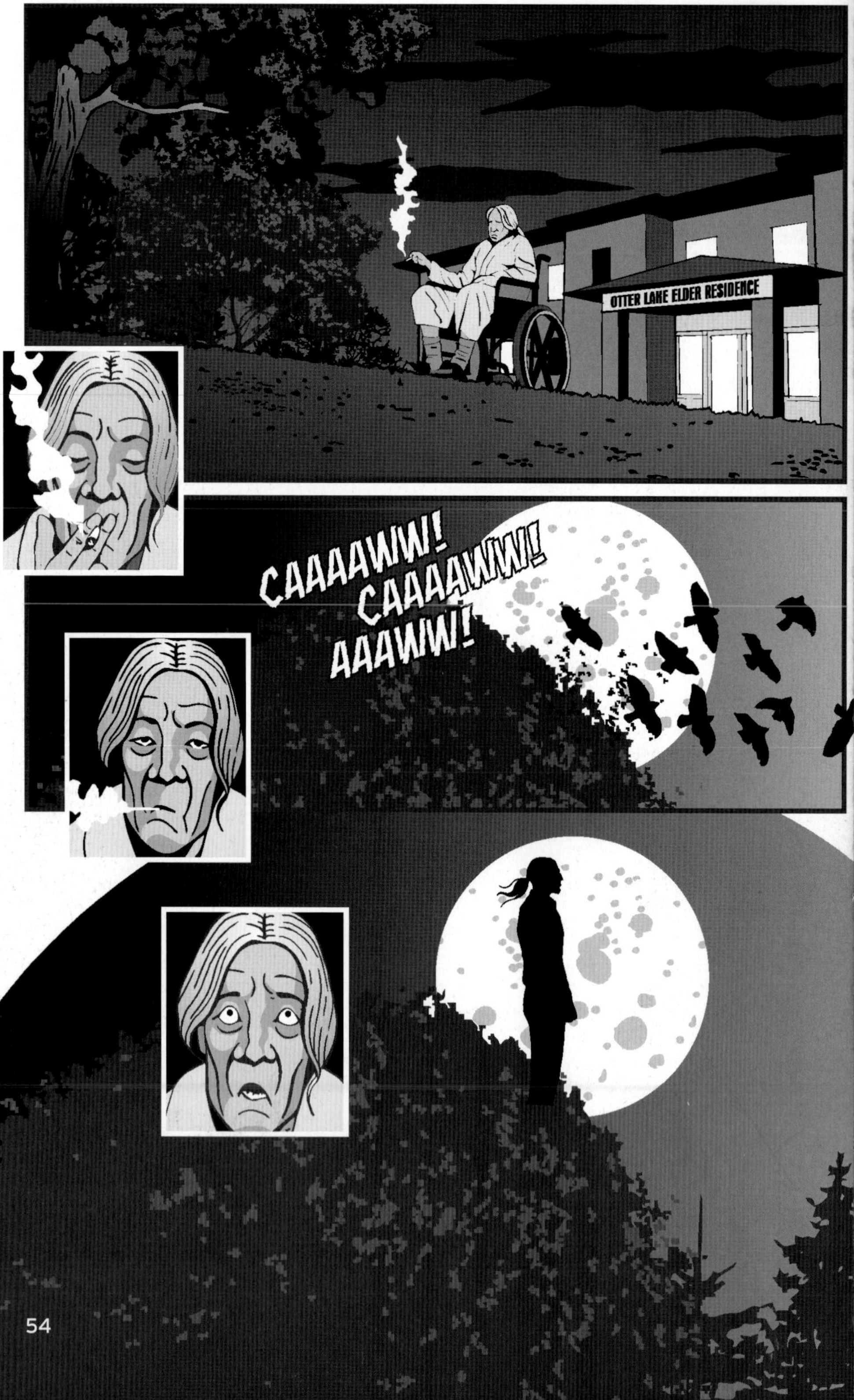
OTTER LAKE ELDER RESIDENCE
CAAAAWW!
CAAAAWW!
AAAWW!

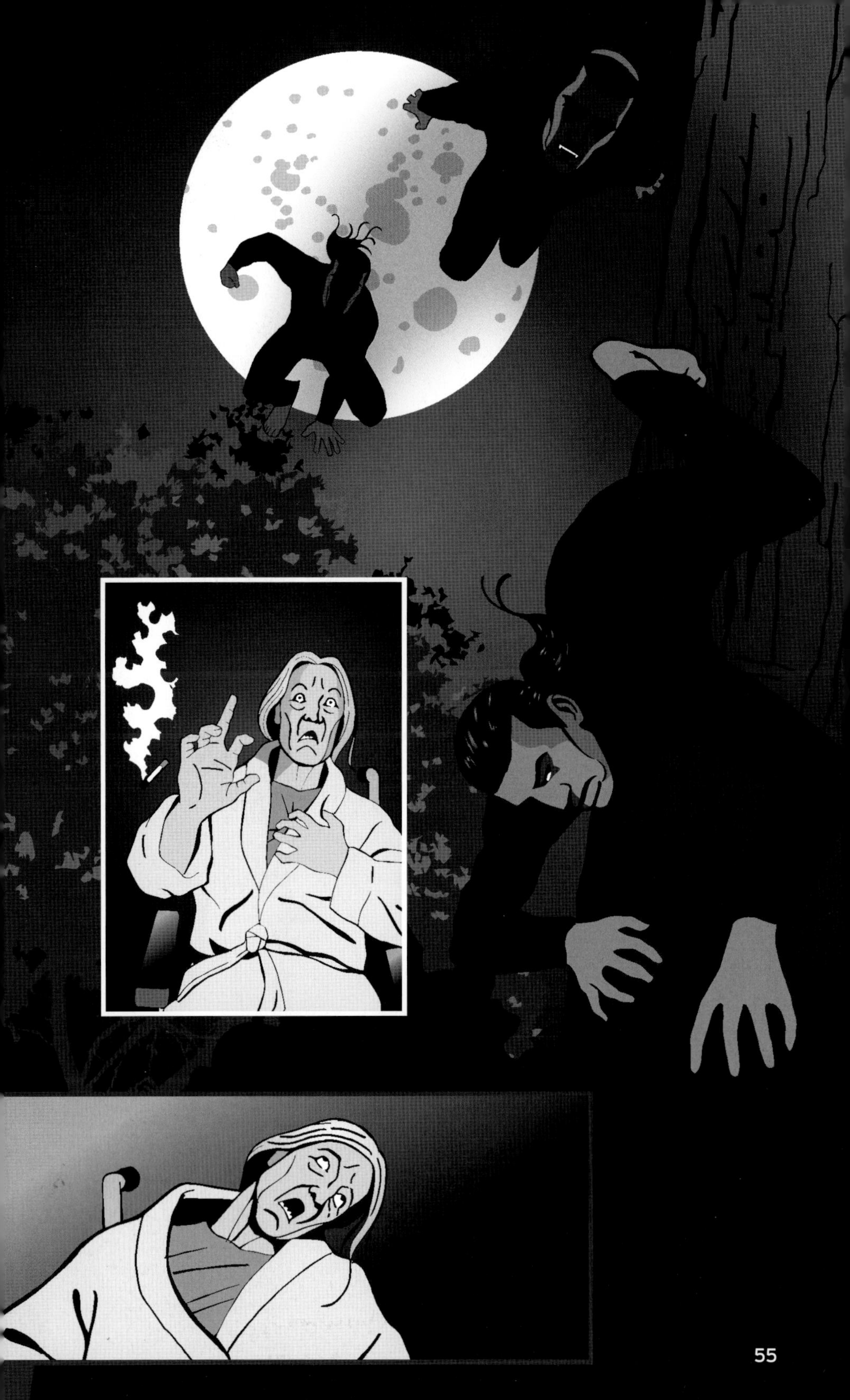

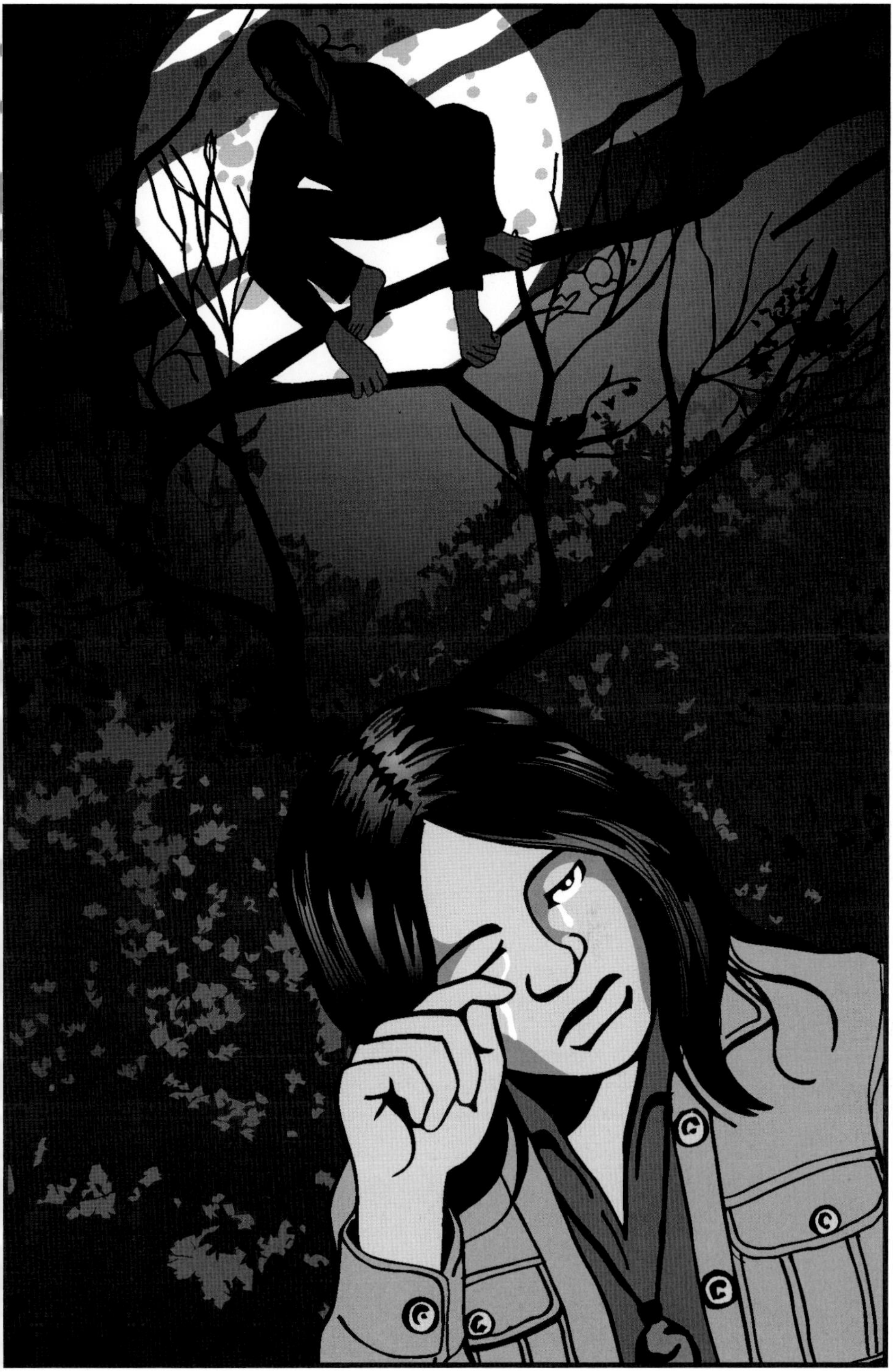

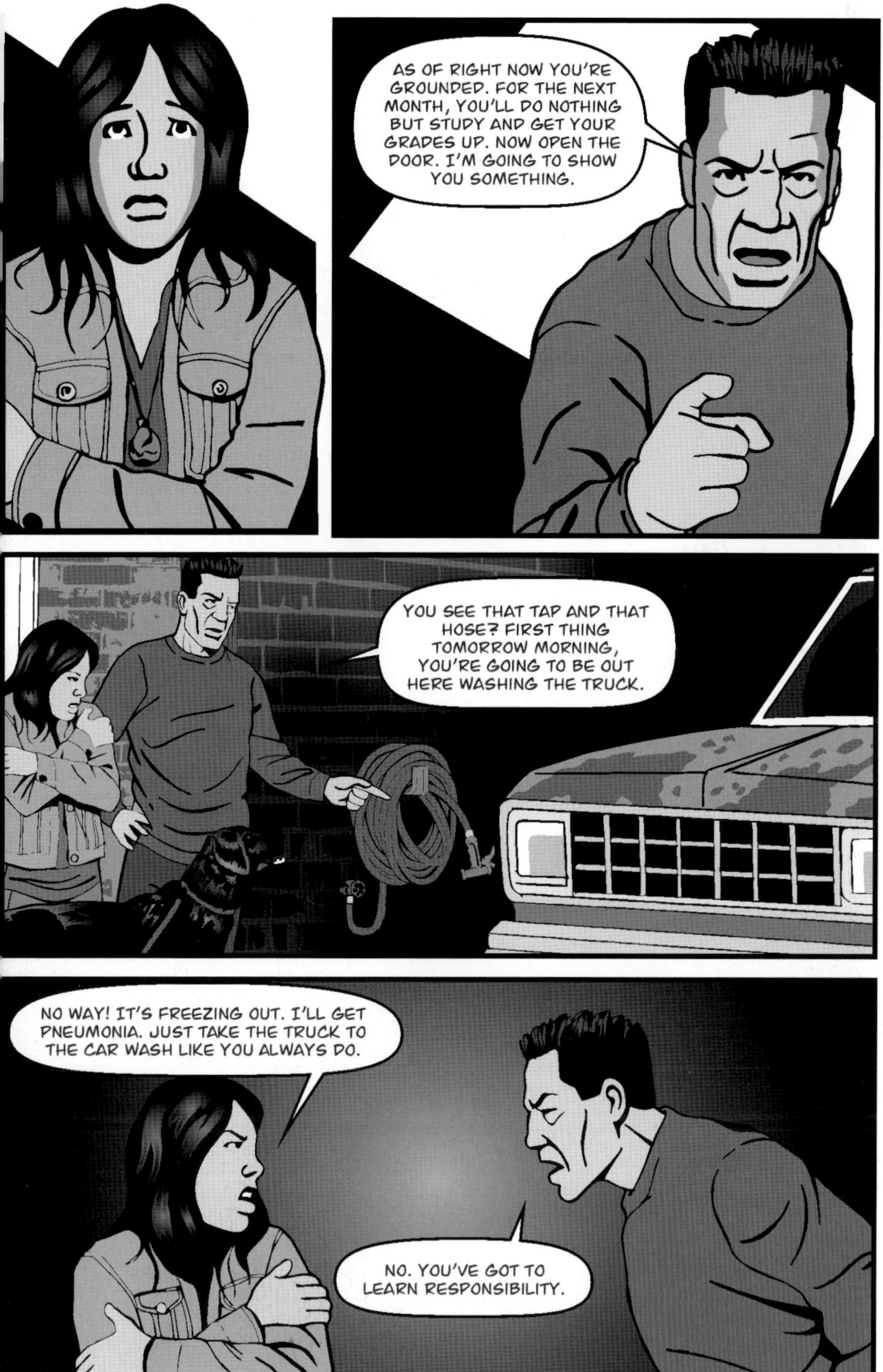
AS OF RIGHT NOW YOU'RE GROUNDED. FOR THE NEXT MONTH, YOU'LL DO NOTHING BUT STUDY AND GET YOUR GRADES UP. NOW OPEN THE DOOR. I'M GOING TO SHOW YOU SOMETHING.
YOU SEE THAT TAP AND THAT HOSE? FIRST THING TOMORROW MORNING, YOU'RE GOING TO BE OUT HERE WASHING THE TRUCK.
NO WAY! IT'S FREEZING OUT. I'LL GET PNEUMONIA. JUST TAKE THE TRUCK TO THE CAR WASH LIKE YOU ALWAYS DO.
NO. YOU'VE GOT TO LEARN RESPONSIBILITY.

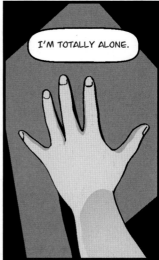

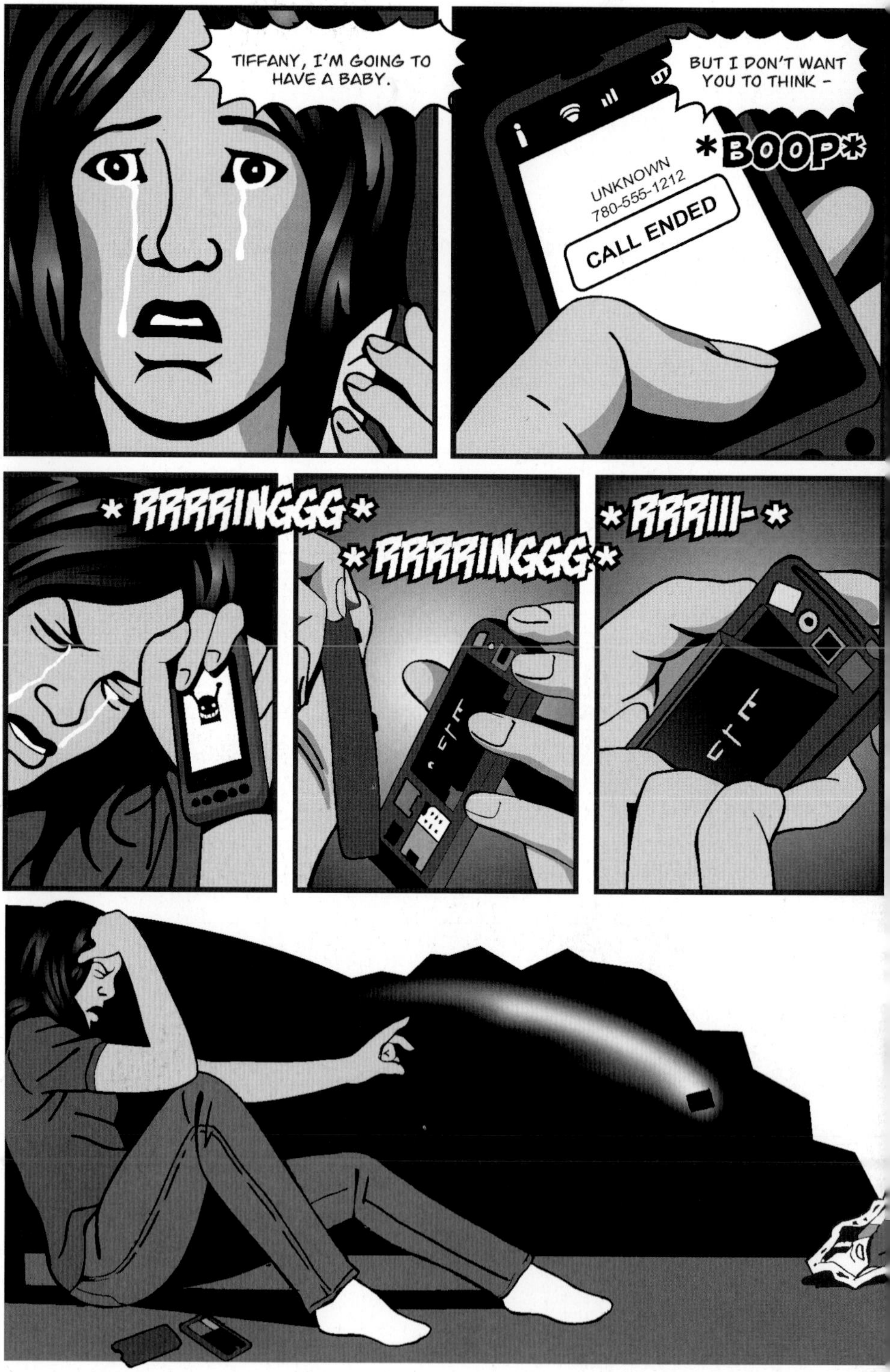
TIFFANY, I'M GOING TO HAVE A BABY.
BUT I DON'T WANT YOU TO THINK -
UNKNOWN
780-555-1212
CALL ENDED
BOOP
* RRRRINGGG *
* RRRRINGGG *
* RRRIII- *

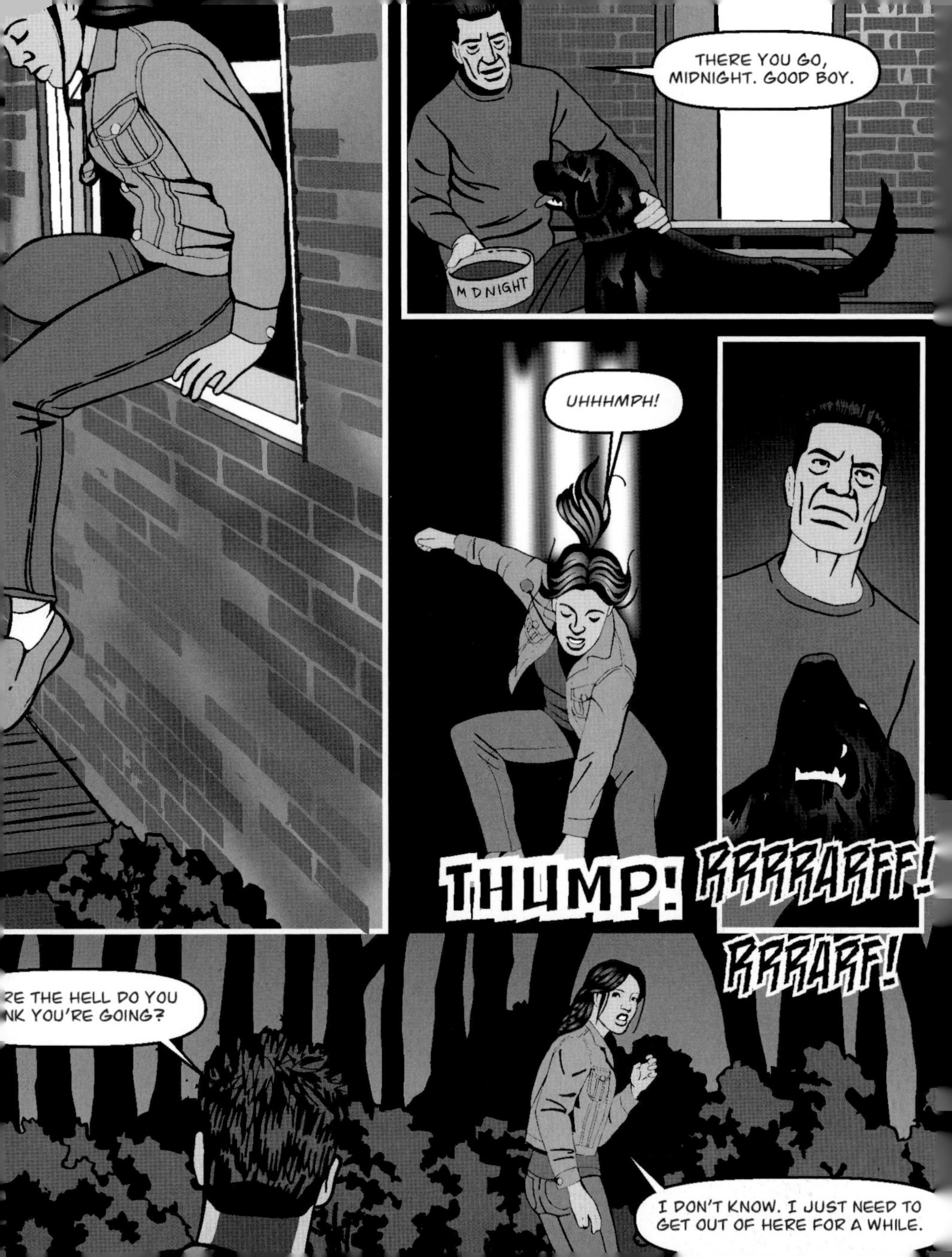
THERE YOU GO, MIDNIGHT. GOOD BOY.
MIDNIGHT
UHHHMPH!
THUMP!
RRRRARFF!
RRRARF!
RE THE HELL DO YOU
NK YOU'RE GOING?
I DON'T KNOW. I JUST NEED TO GET OUT OF HERE FOR A WHILE.

68

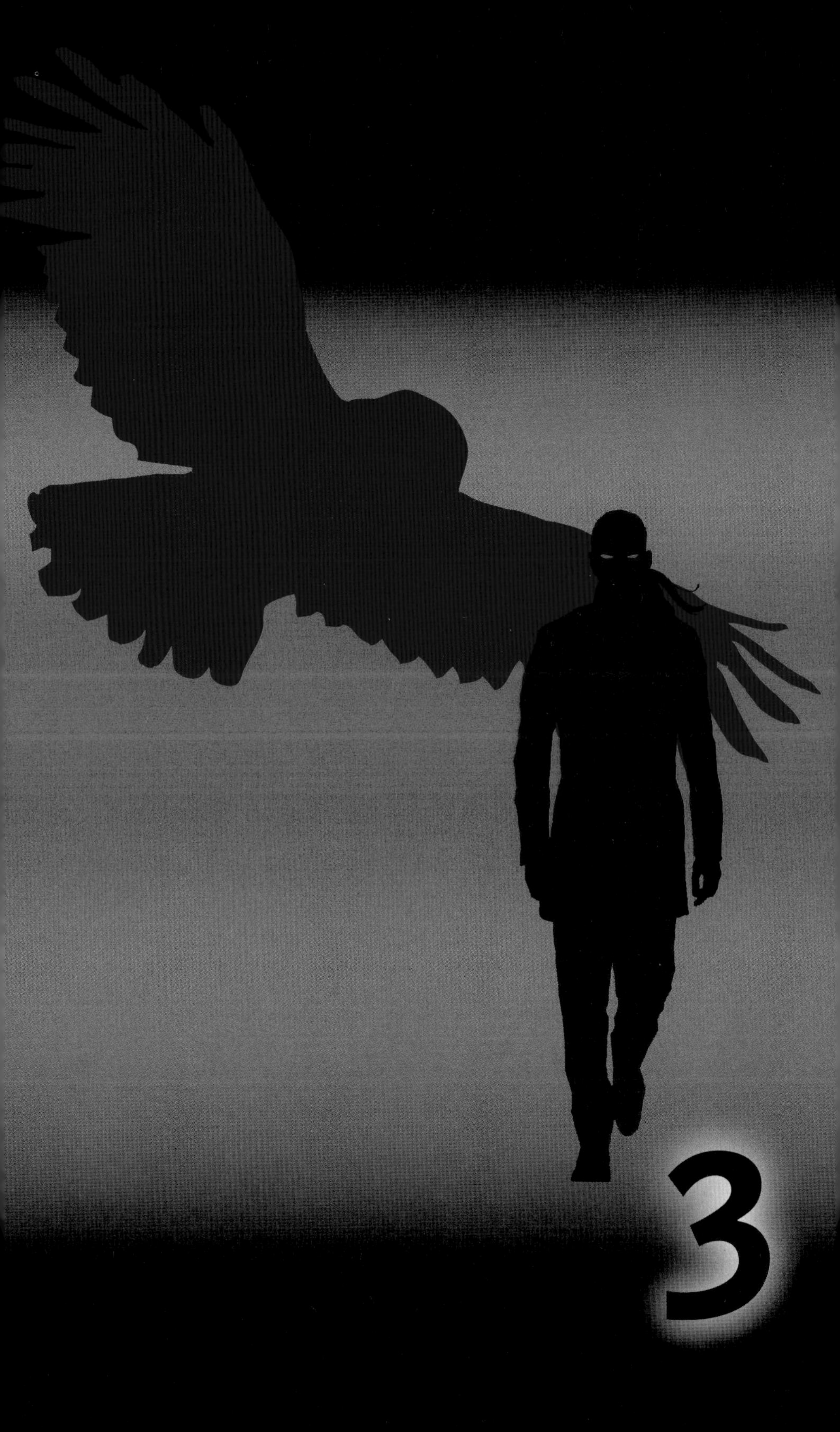
3

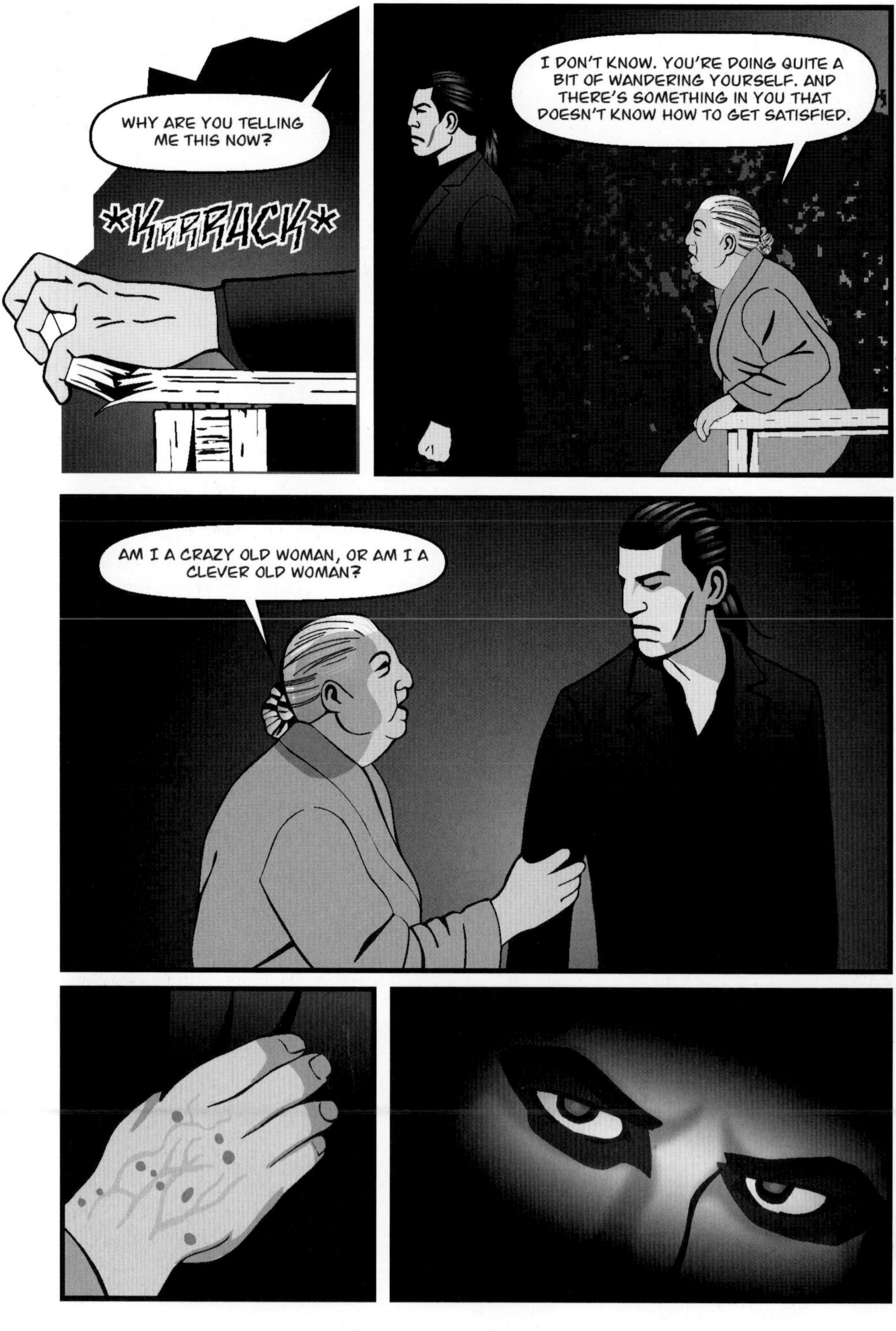
WHY ARE YOU TELLING ME THIS NOW?
KRRRACK
I DON'T KNOW. YOU'RE DOING QUITE A BIT OF WANDERING YOURSELF. AND THERE'S SOMETHING IN YOU THAT DOESN'T KNOW HOW TO GET SATISFIED.
AM I A CRAZY OLD WOMAN, OR AM I A CLEVER OLD WOMAN?

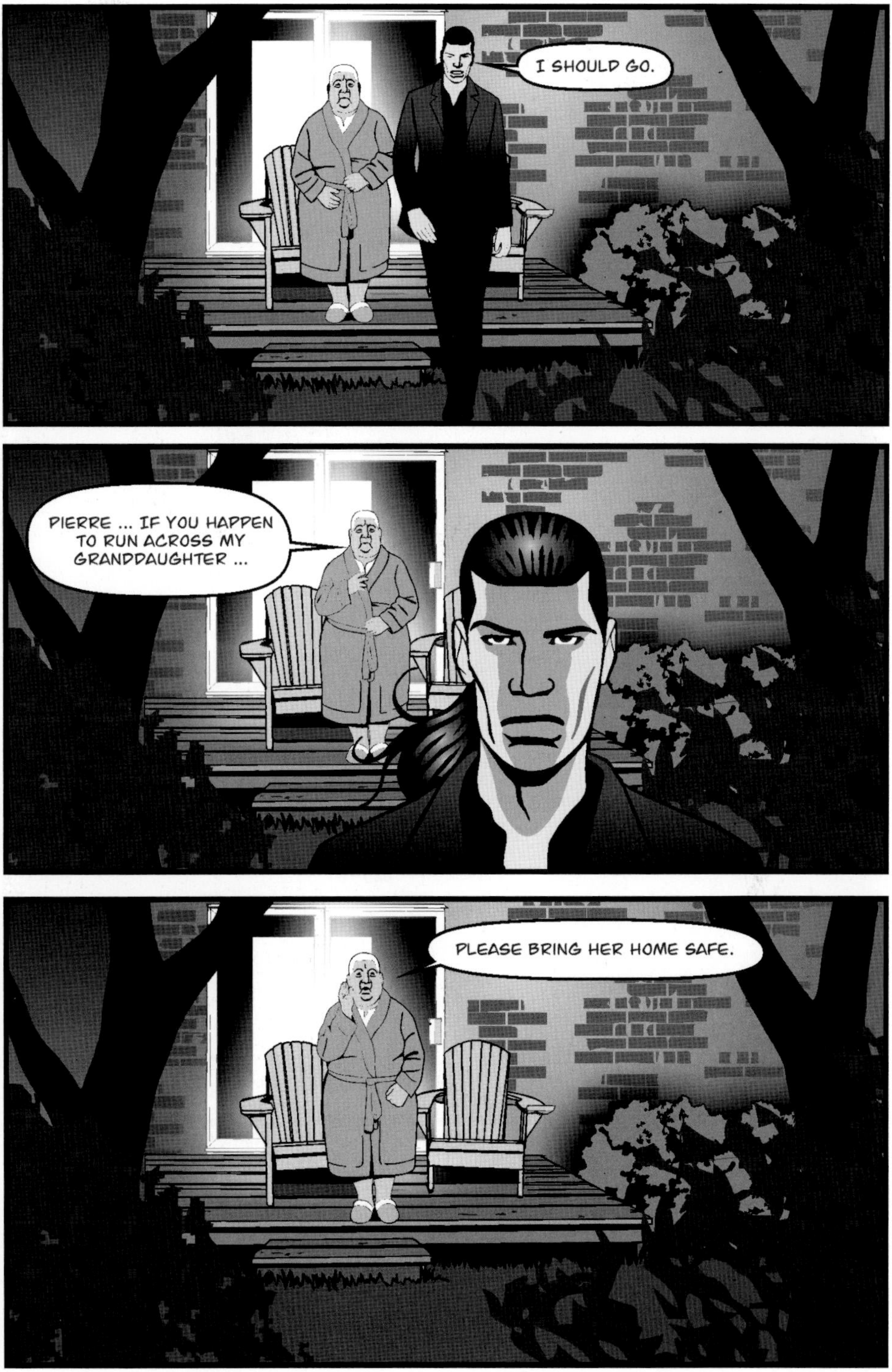
I SHOULD GO.
PIERRE ... IF YOU HAPPEN TO RUN ACROSS MY GRANDDAUGHTER ...
PLEASE BRING HER HOME SAFE.

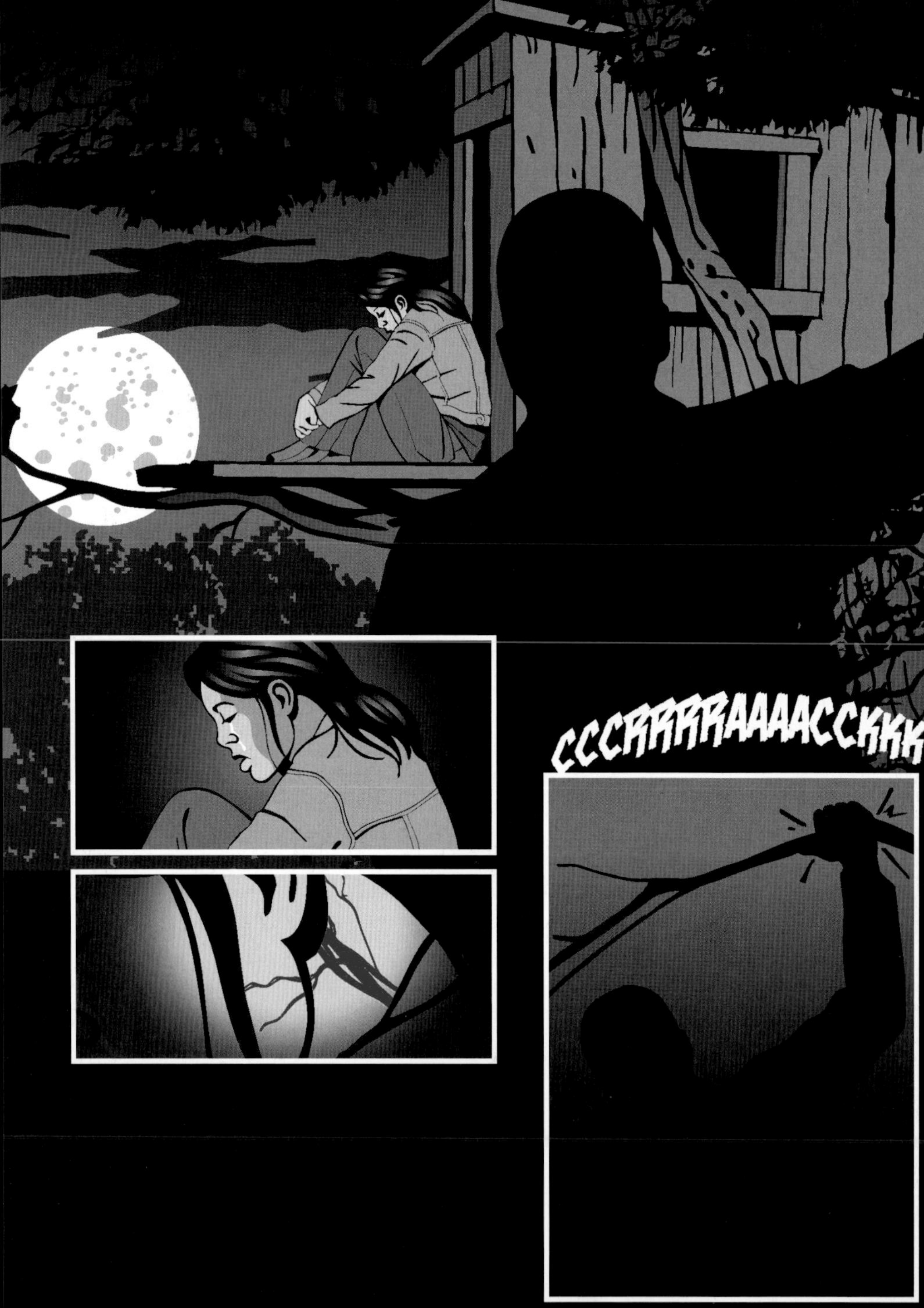
CCCRRRRAAAACCKKK

86

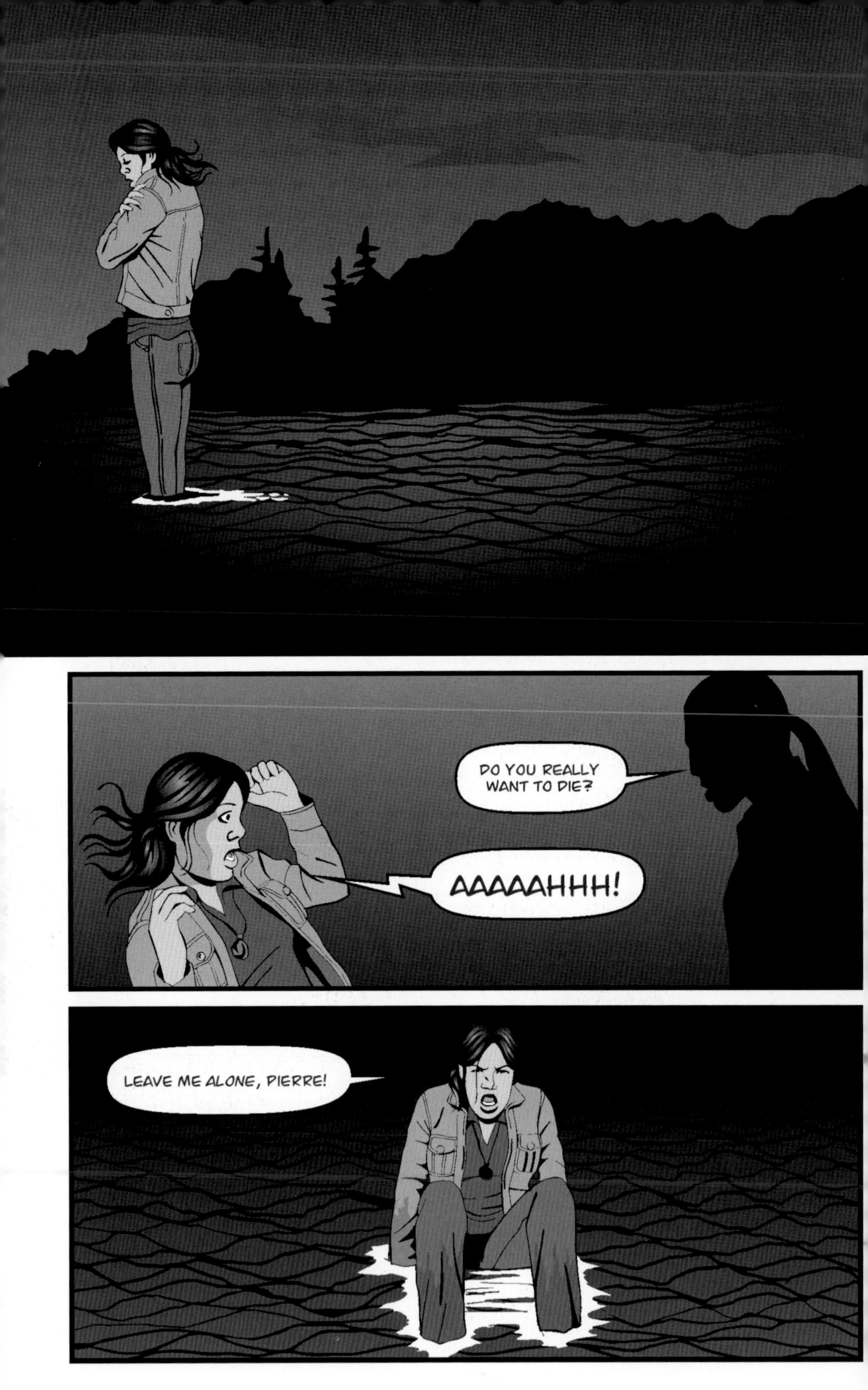
DO YOU REALLY WANT TO DIE?
AAAAAHHH!
LEAVE ME ALONE, PIERRE!

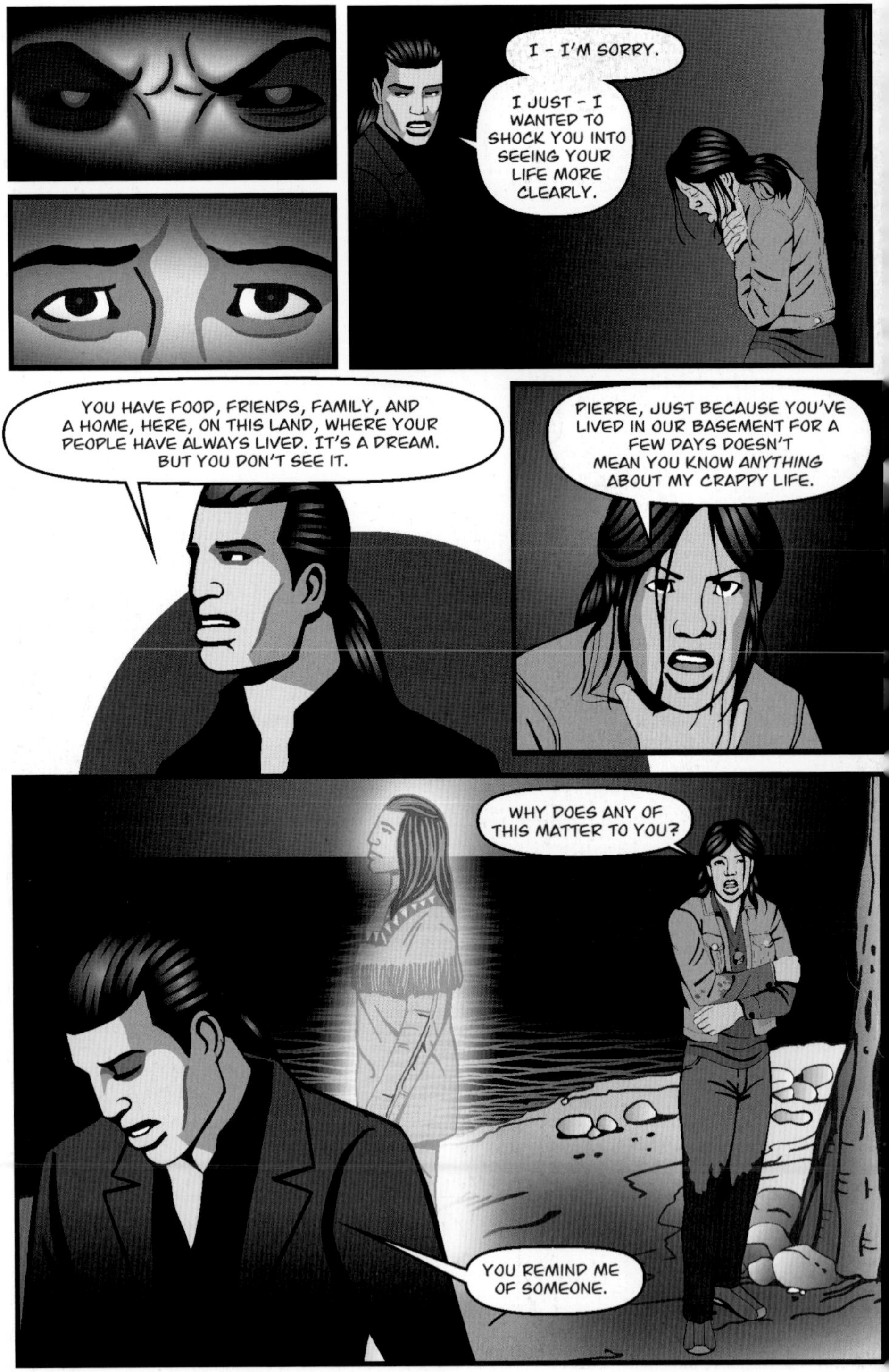
I - I'M SORRY.
I JUST - I WANTED TO SHOCK YOU INTO SEEING YOUR LIFE MORE CLEARLY.
YOU HAVE FOOD, FRIENDS, FAMILY, AND A HOME, HERE, ON THIS LAND, WHERE YOUR PEOPLE HAVE ALWAYS LIVED. IT'S A DREAM. BUT YOU DON'T SEE IT.
PIERRE, JUST BECAUSE YOU'VE LIVED IN OUR BASEMENT FOR A FEW DAYS DOESN'T MEAN YOU KNOW *ANYTHING* ABOUT MY CRAPPY LIFE.
WHY DOES ANY OF THIS MATTER TO YOU?
YOU REMIND ME OF SOMEONE.

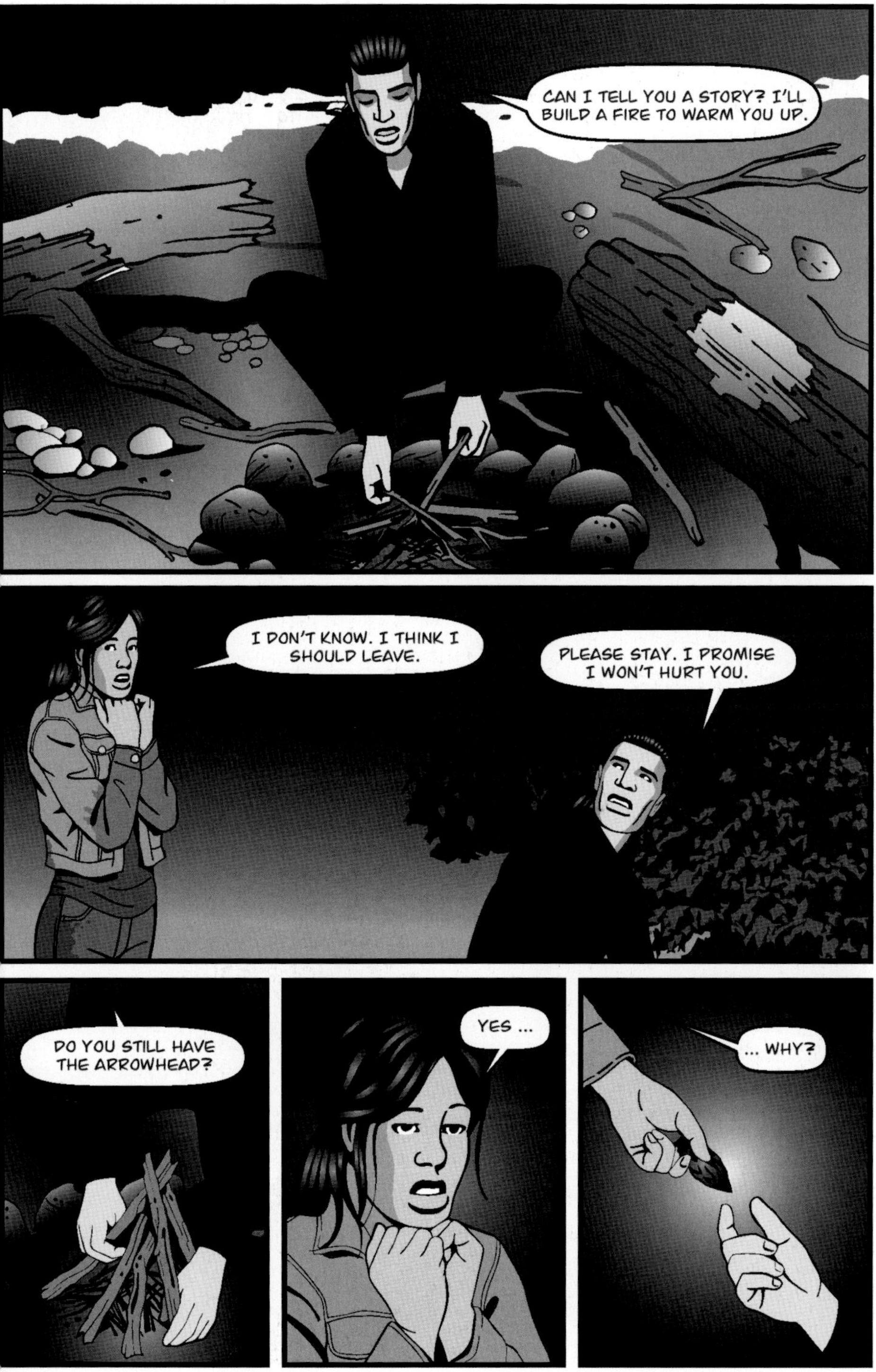
CAN I TELL YOU A STORY? I'LL BUILD A FIRE TO WARM YOU UP.
I DON'T KNOW. I THINK I SHOULD LEAVE.
PLEASE STAY. I PROMISE I WON'T HURT YOU.
DO YOU STILL HAVE THE ARROWHEAD?
YES ...
... WHY?

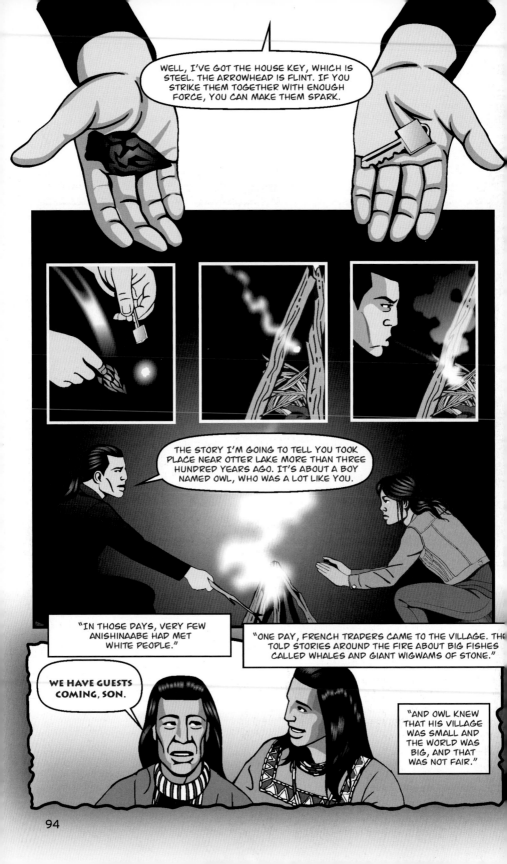

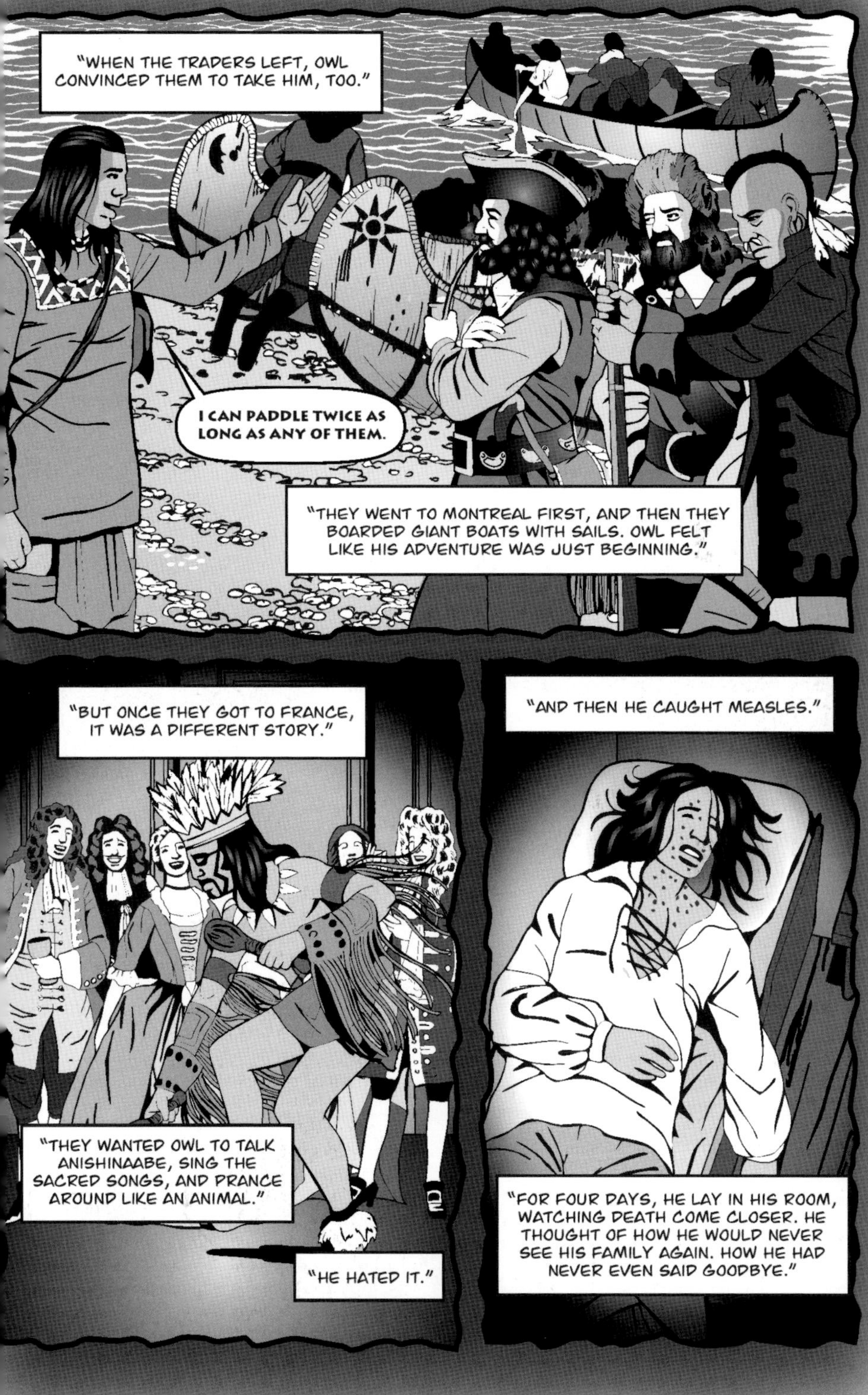
"WHEN THE TRADERS LEFT, OWL CONVINCED THEM TO TAKE HIM, TOO."
I CAN PADDLE TWICE AS LONG AS ANY OF THEM.
"THEY WENT TO MONTREAL FIRST, AND THEN THEY BOARDED GIANT BOATS WITH SAILS. OWL FELT LIKE HIS ADVENTURE WAS JUST BEGINNING."
"BUT ONCE THEY GOT TO FRANCE, IT WAS A DIFFERENT STORY."
"THEY WANTED OWL TO TALK ANISHINAABE, SING THE SACRED SONGS, AND PRANCE AROUND LIKE AN ANIMAL."
"HE HATED IT."
"AND THEN HE CAUGHT MEASLES."
"FOR FOUR DAYS, HE LAY IN HIS ROOM, WATCHING DEATH COME CLOSER. HE THOUGHT OF HOW HE WOULD NEVER SEE HIS FAMILY AGAIN. HOW HE HAD NEVER EVEN SAID GOODBYE."

97

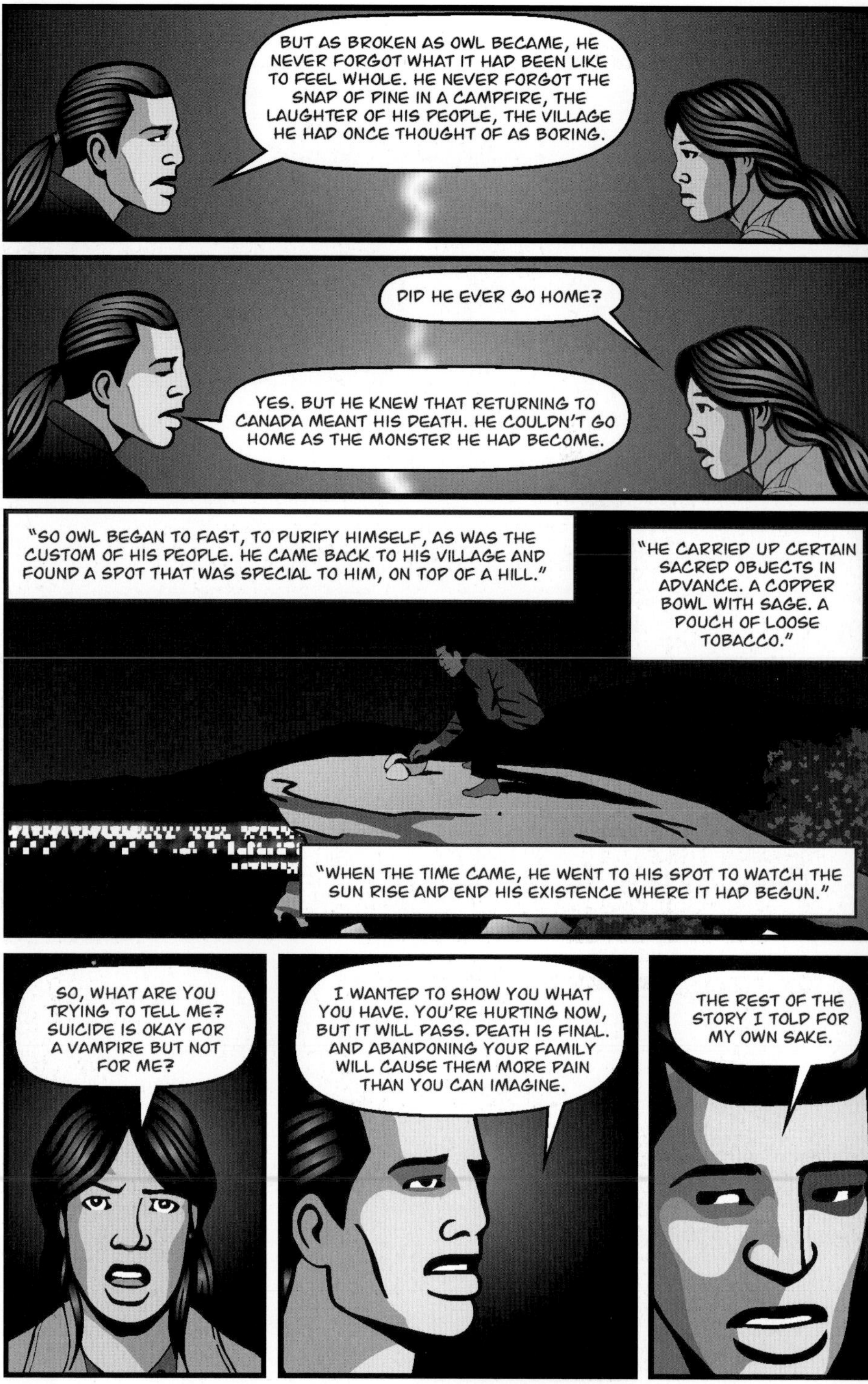
BUT AS BROKEN AS OWL BECAME, HE NEVER FORGOT WHAT IT HAD BEEN LIKE TO FEEL WHOLE. HE NEVER FORGOT THE SNAP OF PINE IN A CAMPFIRE, THE LAUGHTER OF HIS PEOPLE, THE VILLAGE HE HAD ONCE THOUGHT OF AS BORING.
DID HE EVER GO HOME?
YES. BUT HE KNEW THAT RETURNING TO CANADA MEANT HIS DEATH. HE COULDN'T GO HOME AS THE MONSTER HE HAD BECOME.
"SO OWL BEGAN TO FAST, TO PURIFY HIMSELF, AS WAS THE CUSTOM OF HIS PEOPLE. HE CAME BACK TO HIS VILLAGE AND FOUND A SPOT THAT WAS SPECIAL TO HIM, ON TOP OF A HILL."
"HE CARRIED UP CERTAIN SACRED OBJECTS IN ADVANCE. A COPPER BOWL WITH SAGE. A POUCH OF LOOSE TOBACCO."
"WHEN THE TIME CAME, HE WENT TO HIS SPOT TO WATCH THE SUN RISE AND END HIS EXISTENCE WHERE IT HAD BEGUN."
SO, WHAT ARE YOU TRYING TO TELL ME? SUICIDE IS OKAY FOR A VAMPIRE BUT NOT FOR ME?
I WANTED TO SHOW YOU WHAT YOU HAVE. YOU'RE HURTING NOW, BUT IT WILL PASS. DEATH IS FINAL. AND ABANDONING YOUR FAMILY WILL CAUSE THEM MORE PAIN THAN YOU CAN IMAGINE.
THE REST OF THE STORY I TOLD FOR MY OWN SAKE.

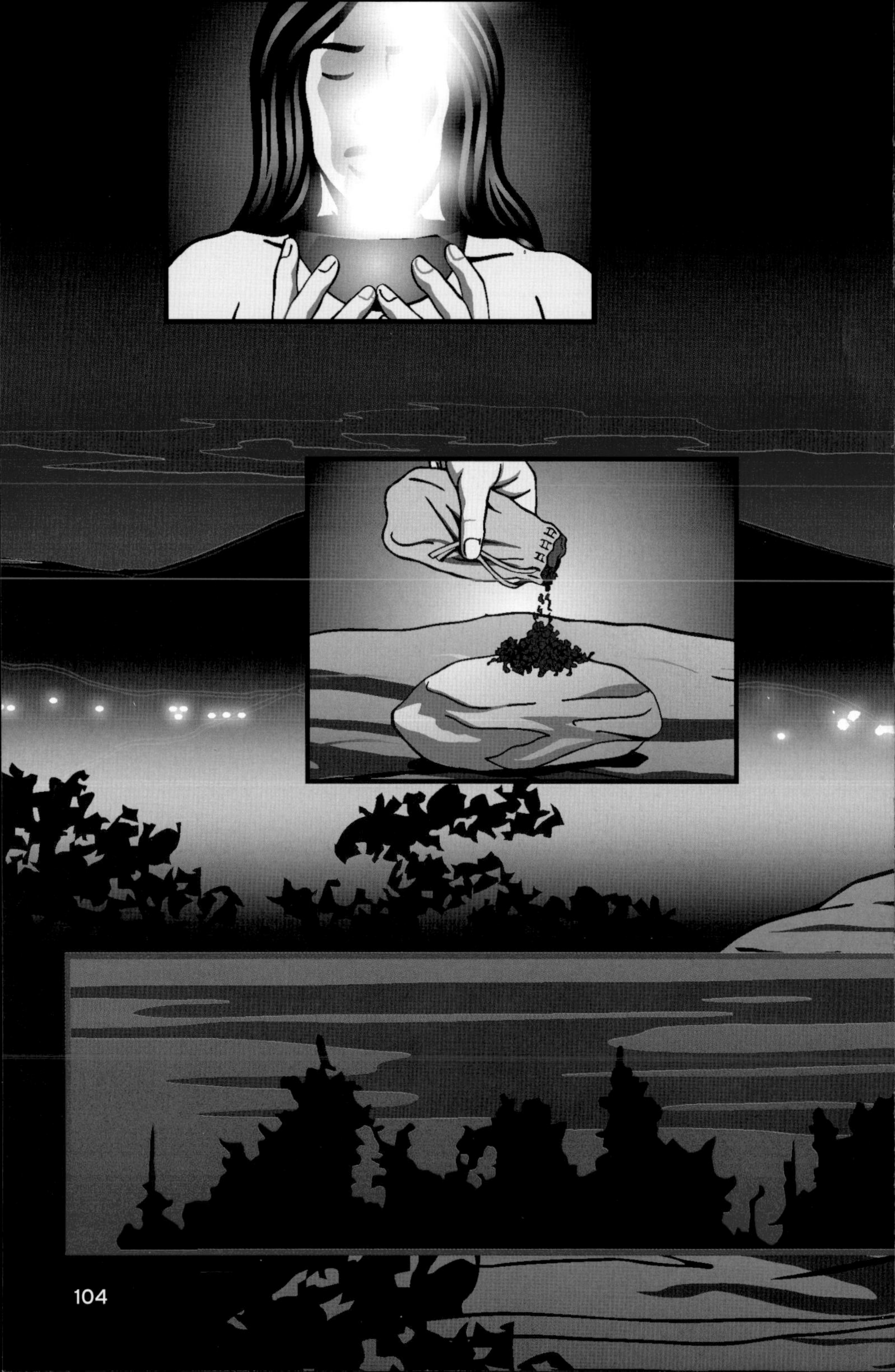

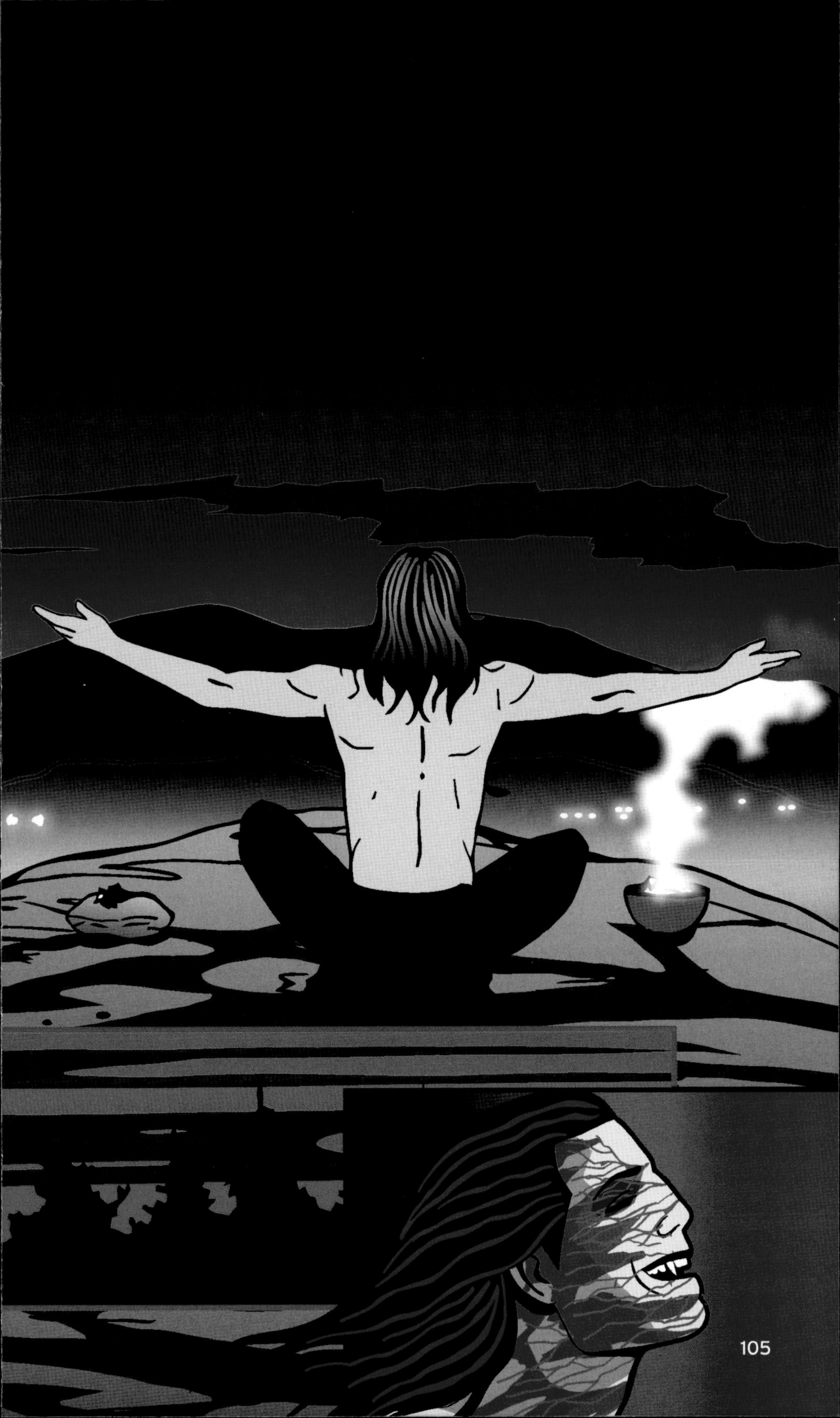

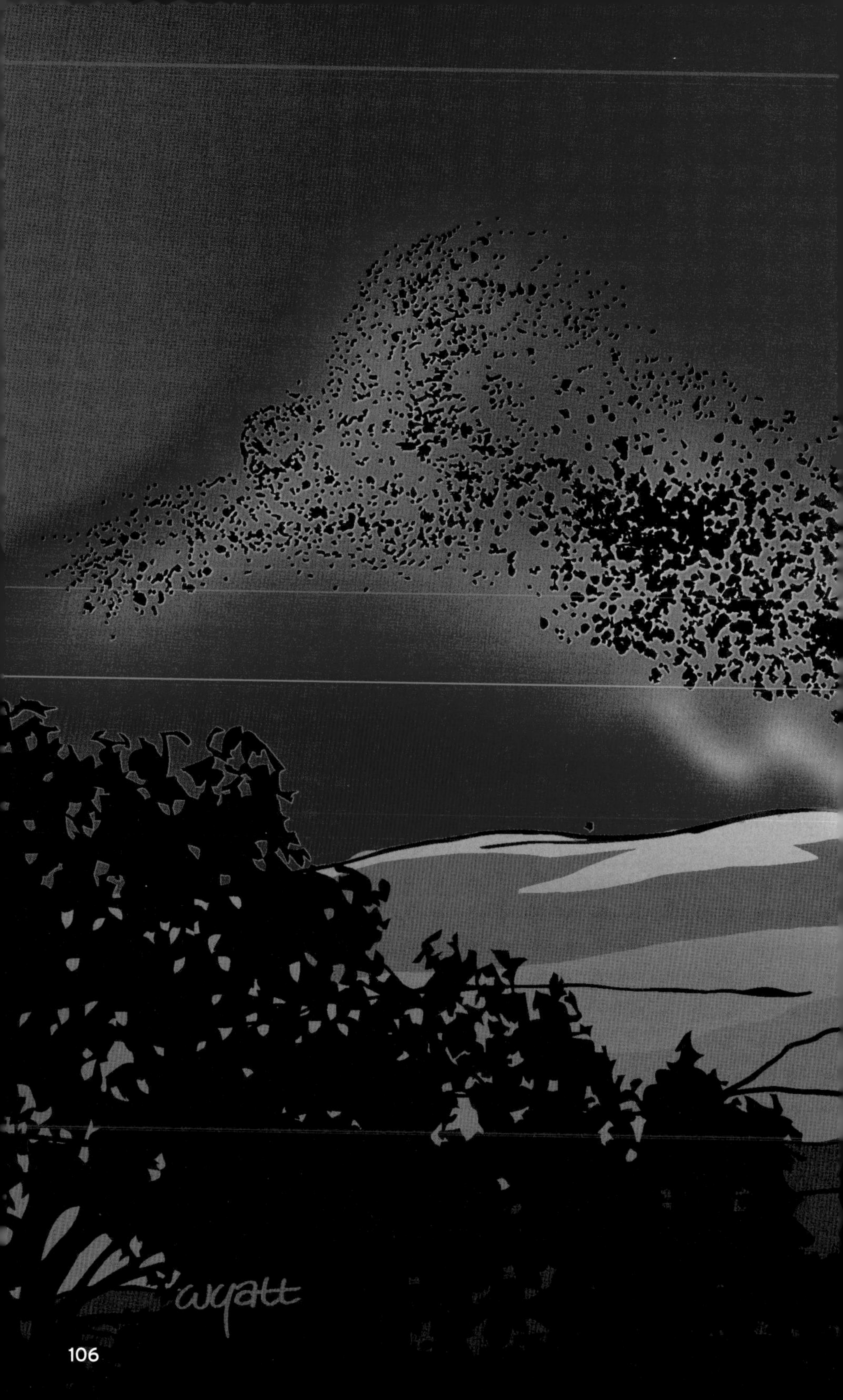
wyatt

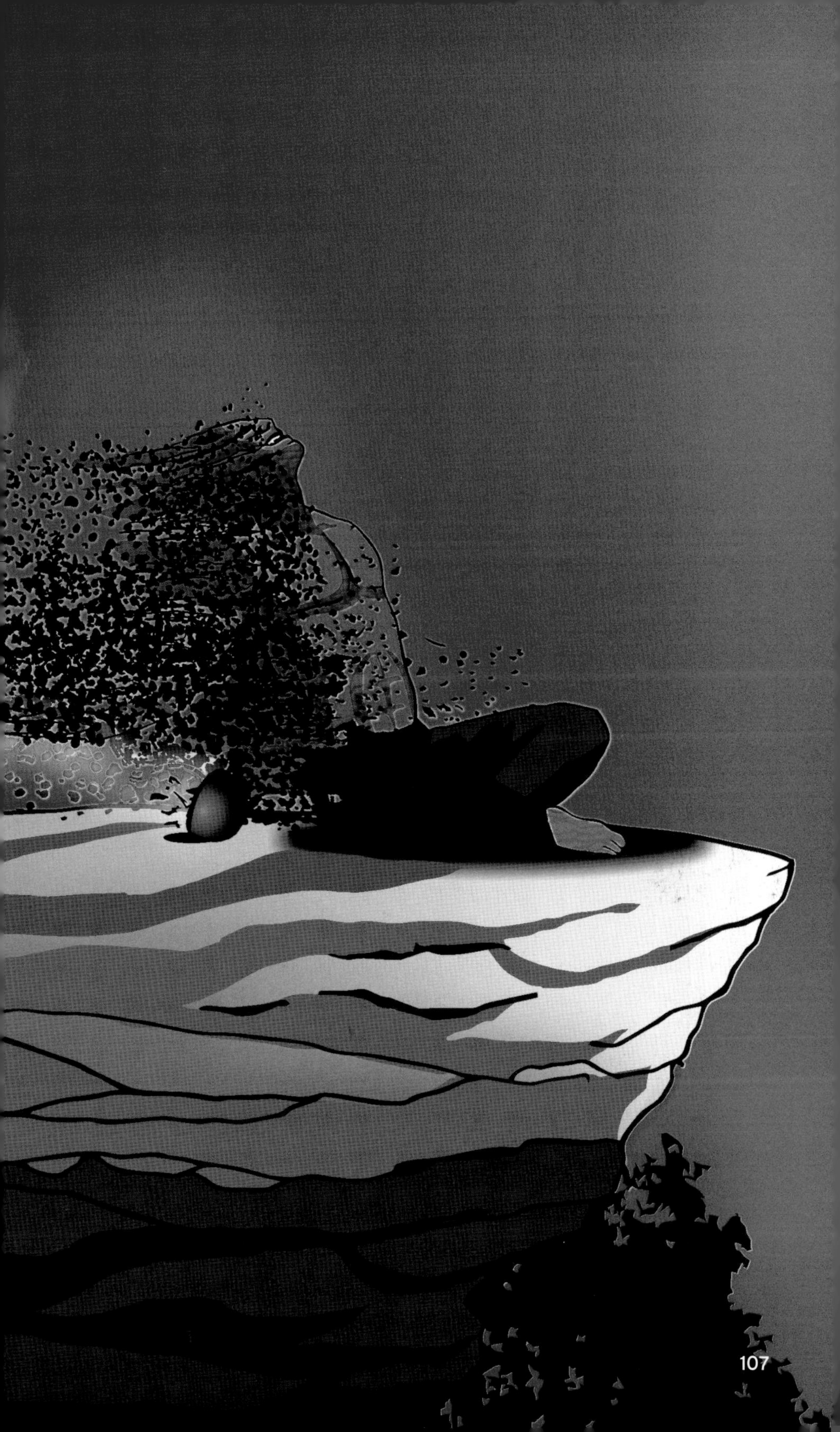

ACKNOWLEDGMENTS

As with most literary creations books are seldom born in a vacuum. Like alchemy, there are many different elements that go into the caldron to synthesize what you hold in your hands.

Therefore, there are many people I would like to thank for making it possible to write this story. *The Night Wanderer* began as a play, *A Contemporary Gothic Indian Vampire Story*, commissioned by Young People's Theatre in Toronto and originally produced by Persephone Theatre in Saskatoon.

From there it lay dormant for a long time. Then Annick Press came knocking on my door about a different project. But you can't keep a good vampire down, it seems (or a good Ojibwa teenager, for that matter).

Fast-forward a year and I find myself sitting in the mountains, at Cabin #4 of the Leighton Studios at the Banff Centre for the Arts. The grant from the Ontario Arts Council also helped foster the creative process.

As well, there are several people who provided valuable research assistance. Trish Warner helped me with various medical details. Tara Redican gave me a good boost by doing some vital early research. A special and fabulous thank you to Janine, who put as much heart and soul into this book as I did. The novel could not have been created without her patience and passion. Many thanks to Aurora Artists for believing in the project as much as I did.

The novel first appeared appeared in 2007. Fast-forward a few more years and it is once again transformed into a graphic novel. I'd like to thank Anne Taylor of the Curve Lake Cultural Centre for her assistance with visual references.

I would also like to thank Anita Knott for her assistance with several of the Ojibwa phrases. And, of course, I offer a hearty thanks to my mother, who thought the simple action of birth allowed me the opportunity to write this book. And to all the Anishinaabe/Ojibwa people in the world.

And to a lesser extent, all the vampires in the world. You know who you are.
—*Drew Hayden Taylor*

A big thank you to all those at Annick Press for their encouragement and enthusiasm.

I would also like to thank Drew Hayden Taylor for his marvelous story and Alison Kooistra for her masterful adaptation.

Lastly, I would like to thank my wife, Janet, and my children, Tyler and Madeline, for their patience, support, and love throughout all those months I spent scribbling away.
—*Michael Wyatt*